BULLY, BULLIED

By Ben Dunn

For my home town

Copyright © 2023

All rights reserved. No part of this publication may be reproduced, distributed, or transmitted in any form or by any means, including photocopying, recording, or other electronic or mechanical methods, without the prior written permission of the publisher, except in the case of brief quotations embodied in critical reviews and certain other non-commercial uses permitted in copyright law. Any references to historical events, real people, or real places are used fictitiously. Names, characters and places are products of the author's imagination.

First printing edition 2023

Book Burn Publishing.

18th May 1990

7.50 a.m.

When it blows there is no hiding. But I'll try because standing there, ignoring the violence, only leads to physical pain.

"Who do you think you are?" my so-called father shouts, his drawl at seven not as slow as it will be later.

He boasts that hangovers never hit, but he lies. The body can't pretend nothing hurts, the impact always there and the mood and the depression and the anger taking the place of headaches, sickness and shakes.

There is no escape without untruths and this man, my laughable role-model, has another reality to mine.

My step-brother, Darren, has pushed with words because he wants the push to be physical. He has chipped and edged and built his way to being a man. His father diminishing as he grew and now the tipping point is near.

But I don't want to watch, not live, it is theirs to do and mine to avoid. But here I am, caught in a room. I am not them, and never can be. Their mass and aggression beyond my control. I am small, wiry to their size, pathetic and weak to their strength.

It hasn't always been the way, my step-dad, the mighty Quinn, is never too shy to hit, threaten or choke. But Darren took it all, and now, the labourer, hitting eighteen and strong and scary, is pushing back, smiling into the face of the man who built him this way, the man who has eroded his physicality with lethargy and booze. The fear he held only palpable in spiteful sounds.

"I'll do what I want," Darren says.

"You'll do what I tell you."

Darren laughs, deep and fake and into his face, walking against the finger in his chest.

"Not any more. What used to be is gone, old man."

Quinn backs down, steps away, not fully, only half a pace. Darren smiles, which is wrong and stupid and not what he has been taught. Quinn whips round, throwing a right hand, short and sharp and down the middle, no round-house swing, a practiced throw and quick and unexpected.

He connects on Darren's chin, staggering him back but not putting him down. But there aren't rules, no counts and no gentleman's nod to the winner. Quinn throws again, the same punch but walking now, pushing bodyweight through his fist and Darren ducks and they clinch, both struggling to lock the other's head. They push through the room, the pine cabinet hit and rocked, but it is empty and only the doors swing open. Darren pushes back and they swear and pull and twist and grab. They hit the pine table, my breakfast of flakes and milk spilling up and over and onto me. I am trapped in a corner, on a pine bench with the men of the house struggling to kill the other.

Quinn drives his hip into Darren's waist, pulling down with the hold he has around Darren's neck. Darren comes up and over, slamming down against a pine chair, his ribs taking the edge of the seat. Quinn kicks out, connecting with Darren's head, and the foot slipping down his cheek and into his shoulder. Quinn raises his foot and stamps down, but Darren is moving and the impact isn't on his temple but on his back. The force drives him down again. Quinn reaches down and wraps his arm around Darren's neck, and he pulls and he presses and he squeezes as Darren's face turns red then purple. Darren passes out, and Quinn lets go and Darren slumps to the floor but wakes on impact.

"You still got a ways to go before you can have me," Quinn says.

Darren looks up, not with it, not ready to go, not ready to fight.

"I'll get there," he says.

"Get out of my house."

"It isn't yours," Darren tells him.

I watch this, what has been building, what was always going to happen, and what will again until Quinn can't do it anymore. He is gasping for air, his lungs not built for exercise, his age not young enough to be risking exhaustion.

Darren stands, unsteady at first and Quinn smiles, ready to throw again. But Darren picks up his bag and walks out the front door, slamming it shut behind him.

I'm not related by blood and not connected through love. This man, big Quinn, a diminished mound of stupidity. The man I fear, the man no one respects and the man I can only hate. This is what I have. This is what I am.

I've just seen that the old man still has it. The panic and sweat on his face says he isn't sure his reign will last.

I am standing, wanting to leave, wanting out of the room and the house, and away from this fool.

"What are you looking at?" he shouts at me.

The answer is the floor, the space, the future, the emptiness. But he doesn't care, it is a madness brought on from humiliation, and while I know tensing makes it worse, makes it hurt that little bit more, I do it all the same.

He drives his clenched right fist from down low and on and up into my ribs on the left side, catching those that float, those that bend, and those that carry the force through to my lungs, and force the air out and the pain to shoot up. I can't help but make a squeal.

"Sound like a girl," he tells me as I sink to my knees, unable to breath, unable to speak and unable to leave.

He never throws combinations, he has only ever hit me twice in succession, and that because I tried to move away from the first. I take the blow, I show him the effects of his strength, power, superiority and manliness. And his world, that awful place he resides watching energy fade away and time get thrown to waste, balances out, or at least stops shaking so he can inflate his ego back toward the delusional place it was when he woke.

My mum shouts, tells him to leave me alone, which is the start and end of her caring. Her face scarred with red capillaries that have swelled and burst and marked her to show all who she is and what is important. She will put her foundation on to hide them all, but they show through, they can be seen, they just don't pulse like they would were you to see her, as I do now, in her natural state.

I don't know who she was, and I don't know my father. I don't think she does either. It isn't Quinn, and that is all that matters.

She smiles as if asking to thank her for saving me. This is her level of care, her level of love, her means to show me her heart: walking Quinn away after he has inflicted damage, so they can spend time together and he doesn't waste energy or emotion on me. A woman I have to call my Mother, because biology says she is. A woman who chose many things, and many people before she thought of me. Chasing whatever it is she thinks she will find at the bottom of a bottle of rum, at the end of her day and in the meaning of life. Quinn stays around, which isn't the normal way of things, not the normal way at all.

He leaves the room, not wanting to watch my weakness as I try not to cry, try not to sob with either the pain, the humiliation or an anger I cannot bring to be anything other than hurtful words directed at a life I do not want.

I don't say goodbye, or see you later, because I hope and pray that I won't. At least not alive. A stroke, or a heart attack, or walking into a road and being hit by truck or car or anything that will maim him. That is something that would make me believe in justice, a painful ruin of the Indian summer Quinn has entered.

I always leave without saying goodbye. This isn't anger or punishment or an attempt at feeling better about the pain in my side, this is what I do: sneak out, walk away and stay away as long as I can. I have my Sports kit, which hasn't been washed this term. I'd do it, I would, but were Quinn to discover I was using the washing machine then abuse and insults follow. It isn't a man's place, it isn't a man's role. My mother doesn't do much, and a PE kit is of no concern to anyone. In a string-pull bag with shorts, and socks and trainers too small. The clothes fit, but they didn't when they were bought. Five years of the same clothes and only now do they seem the right size.

I close the front door quietly behind me, and stand on the third step of the council house I live in. The area outside is huge and green, and mostly grass, not cut short. A large tree is at the border between us and the street. I am walking out in my school uniform. My white shirt is grey, and looks worse each week as separating the colours is not something my mother does. My shoes are good, a charity shop buy, someone else's initial's inside. My blazer too small, sleeves too high on my arms, and bought new by somebody else, someone smaller than me. I know how I look but I learned not to think.

I am late, avoiding the busiest times. The street empty of kids because they have all already gone. I think about walking away, into the woods where I have spent days from school and no one caring, no one phoning home. It wouldn't matter, no one answers. I don't even know if we are connected anymore.

After ten, the pair of them will be juiced up, gone to the world and believing their life is the one they need for happiness. Wasted hours, wasted lives with their wasted bodies on a bed of large clear and empty vodka bottles.

I'm happy no one is around, no one to stare or talk or joke or taunt. I like it that way. But I know what they are thinking because I can hear what they say. And I am all those things, and more. Some because of what I have done and said, others because of what my brother has threatened and caused. I can't escape being the next one along. I can't escape the brand I have burned into my life by having the name of a Greegan, Billy Greegan, the youngest of them all.

It's a thirty-minute walk, and the register will be taken in twenty minutes time. I think and debate about what to do and where to go. At school I am safe in a way, although not as much as authority thinks. I'm safe from being undiscovered, safe from beatings Quinn might make, free from hiding in my own house. But I'm not free from them, the kids and the teachers, not free from their looks and their words and their idea of me and who I am. I can't break free of that. I can't change either. There is nothing to move to, but if I am honest there is nothing to move from.

I'm average height for an adult female, but being a teenage boy, this makes me short. I'm skin and bone or streaky and weak, depending on how you look. I hear the words, look like you need a good meal on a regular, and they are right, I do. My shaven head just adds to the prisoner look.

The street is long, and at the base of a valley. It isn't quite the lowest part as that is for the river. But it is close enough to have houses only on one side. They are mostly bungalows built a long time ago when men had just won wars and they needed to come back and live a life they believed would mean something. I hope they did as maybe that means that someday I can too.

Cars line both sides of the street, one with a drop down to water, the other a six-foot brick wall broken every ten paces by steps up into a garden and property and view. From the estate where I live, this is the main road to anywhere you may need to go. Town, school, the sea-front or pub, you have to pass this way. The other side has a hill slipping easily down into the town, past coach carparks and the train station. It takes money to live over there, and the town sure has a lot.

I think of Darren and Quinn, the struggle, the slaps, the punches thrown, the red faces and the headlocks. I've seen it before in school, kids wanting to emulate fighters of gym-trained skill but looking like the feeble nothings they are. Punches thrown, rarely connect and then a scuffle, a wrestle, each in headlocks or just the one and then a time-limit reached, the separation of the two and anger lingering. Darren hadn't been smart, hadn't thought, hadn't planned, not well. He should have waited, let Quinn drink, let him fall into the stumbles and bumps of the man who cannot stand let alone fight. Darren should have waited, left the physical to when he had all the advantage. Quinn as a drunk couldn't defend himself, wouldn't be able to breathe, not with his nicotine lungs all covered in tar. Darren blew it, but he'll come again, that much is certain. Quinn knows it, and he'll try to stop it by making Darren leave. But he needs to do it quick because the time is coming.

What happens then, I don't want to know. Quinn won't leave, my mum wouldn't allow it. She would have a choice, the house is hers. And that is no choice. Quinn stays and everyone else be damned. I touch my side, feel the pain, the bruise that is forming, the swelling that is up. I smile, not in fun or in hope, just that I am me, and this is what I have, and it is so absurd.

8.45 a.m.

The school is built on a long winding hill. Three separate sites, separated by green fields. The lower down the hill you go, the older the kids become. Form groups move down. But classes are mixed throughout. There are four gyms of old wooden floors, and wooden wall equipment. The buildings built around a hub of the old red brick and fanning out into solid thick white painted stone. Parts look posh, like some school that has cloisters and students with top hats, while other places have wood-panelled temporary huts to cope with an overflow of kids that have been and gone. Any age of education visible somewhere on site.

There are multiple ways in, like an old town fortress with gates spread around its perimeter. I am looking across a busy road, one with trucks and cars and motorbikes coming down at speed and trundling up in low gear. The old-man with his pole and sign to stop cars killing students, and his bright orange jacket is stood, waiting, nothing to do. He sees me and walks out into an empty road, stopping imaginary traffic, and ushering me across.

"You're late," he says, with a smile and his grey thinning hair under the military style cap he wears.

A man who has come full-circle. If he wasn't a student here back when he was young, he would have been somewhere. He would have been the little kid chasing across a road to get to registration, maybe with friends, or maybe like me, alone. He would have led a life, done whatever he could, and now he is back, the sentinel to many generations after, standing as the young ridicule him, or ignore him, or look at him with contempt. Minimum wage, not for covering costs but for something to do. And soon, when exams come and go, and I write my name and not much else, I will be out there, no law to say I have to learn, I must not work. Just the obligation to contribute to a house where money is wasted on things I will not do. Maybe it won't be so long before I am back, working at a school I never really attended.

I smile and nod and say nothing as I reach the other side and the main gate into the oldest part of the school, with its drive and small island roundabout, and the carpark with the cars of the important staff. The head, the assistants, the big boys and girls that have been here long enough to be people making decisions and demanding respect. I don't know a lot of their names but I know they will have heard of mine.

One town, one school, a thousand students from all around and my crime is being a Greegan.

But that hasn't always been the way. I was born a Taylor as that is my mother's maiden name. A Taylor, which is nothing special, nothing to fear, nothing to associate with violence, stupidity or crime. Not a rich name, not a poor one either, non-descript with no connotations to anything other than England. But I was given Greegan at age eight. Quinn arrived, the world changed, more people arrived and my smile dissolved. I can't say if I was happy before, or just too young and ignorant. I remember being free, whether that is good or bad I cannot say. I was me, my mum was there, I knew nothing else. There were men who came and went, none of whom I could describe or remember. They were there, but never permanent. And I was just someone they wanted to make smile and laugh at jokes. Even Quinn to start, I think, I remember that.

They married, I took the name, officially or not I couldn't say. And in an instant, I became someone else, someone less. To me that is, to others I don't think I changed at all. A new name for an old problem, a different way of calling me nothing, extra reasons for believing I was destined to be forgotten.

8.50 a.m.

"Good of you to join us," Mr. Crane says.

There is no humour but the class laugh all the same. It is best to stay on his good side. A small man with heels on his shoes desperate for the power.

He is standing at the front of the class, his blonde hair blown into shape, a quiff of exact design, and his three-piece suit, the jacket over his chair, his blue sleeves rolled up and his waist-coat done up. I am sure he would love a pocket watch on a chain so he could look at it and tut when students walk in minutes after they should. There is a blue folder in front of him, the names all checked, mine with the standard black dot of absence. He is older than me but younger than Quinn. And like us both he is no man at all.

"Any excuses?" he asks, desperately wanting to show his verbal expertise against me, the kid who never speaks.

I shake my head and walk to the desk that he allocated as mine. It is at the back, in the corner, as far from him as is possible in the space of this English room. The table is for two, but it is only mine. No one needs to sit with me.

"What was that?" he asks.

I have said nothing, and made no sound but I stop my pacing, I turn to him. I look at the smug little face, the guy who is here because ultimately anywhere else he'd be nothing. He stares into people's eyes, not blinking, and this is his way to intimidate. He is always looking up.

Today I stare back, I have looked at the floor too much already. My side hurts.

"A difficult morning," I say, and he laughs.

"Difficult? Everyone else turned up on time. Do you think theirs weren't difficult?"

Because we are all the same experiencing the same, and it is on us to ignore and pretend and follow the rules.

"I couldn't care less if they were or weren't," I say, pulling my chair out.

"And that is your problem right there," he shouts.

"No, my problem is arseholes."

A few students dare to giggle, not through humour but through fear. They are scared of a reaction they expect but rarely see.

He tip-toes and bellows.

"Don't bother with the chair. Get yourself to Mr. Hutton's office, tell him I sent you. Explain why you are late. Explain what you said."

I stare at him because I don't understand the way he works, the beliefs he has. The rules are the rules around here, not like other places. Not like my home. The major one is to just agree and nod and do what they say and accept the idea he is right, always, and I am wrong and that whatever is going on is of no concern. Timekeeping is where it is all at, just like making my bed will change my existence from unbearable to bliss. It is stupid but peddled as a theory that works.

I push my chair back, it makes a noise, a screech. Kids laugh, I don't know why.

"Now," Mr. Crane shouts.

8.55 a.m.

Mr. Hutton is a head of year. Always mine, he followed us through. He has an office, he has a secretary, or at least that's what she seems to be. She sits at a desk outside his room, acting as a filter for the idiocy he just can't be bothered to face without constraint.

I walk in without knocking, and she looks up and smiles. She has it perfected, that instant appraisal of who you are and how you feel, knowing in a glance what approach to take, what face to pull, what words to use. She should teach this, and maybe she does, to colleagues who couldn't pick up on any emotion even if I was shoving a gun in their face.

"Hey Billy," she says.

There is no William for her, no Will or anything else. Billy, all friendly and close.

"Any reason you are here?"

"Mr. Crane."

She makes the sound of someone who has been told the answer to a question and needs no further explanation. Where is Richard? Broke his leg. Ah. The implication is already there, no need for further details. He won't be coming. Ah.

Mr. Crane. Ah. Words and sounds that fit together with ease.

"Late?" she asks.

I nod. "And swearing."

"Good ones?"

"Arsehole."

She smiles.

"Could be worse."

"Wanted it to be."

She smiles again and points at a chair. I need to sit and wait for her boss, and mine to talk.

She picks up a phone and presses a button.

"It's Billy," she says. "Late and swearing." She pauses. "Arsehole." She laughs. "Ok," she finishes.

She looks at me.

"Take your book," she tells me, pointing at the shelf to my right.

The room is old, and like a school and made of wood. Panels, shelves, tables and chairs. All dark and all matching. But of a different time when teachers wore cloaks and those silly flat hats.

I could have walked, could have not come here at all. It wouldn't have been the first time, but maybe I have already done it the last. I could have walked out the gate, which is always open. One of the many. They don't lock us in, they don't patrol the routes. There is an implicit agreement that if you don't want to be here you can go. So I have, many times. As long as it isn't obvious, or loud, or destructive, strolling out and not coming back is easy to do. Most kids leave at lunchtime and hang out in the town, buying food, or whatever they want with the money their parents give. My meals are free, but I have to be here for them. Free school meals, which is chips, and possibly a cornflake cake. I'm hungry a lot.

The book she is telling me to pick up is History. Mr. Hutton loves the past, probably the present too. I have no idea about his thoughts on the future, at least not for him. He speaks about what could and will happen in assemblies, in chats, and when he shouts to reprimand the idiots that infest this place. The future is where it is at, what are you going to do? What do you think you can achieve? Do you not want a better one for yourself? They sound like the warning words of a man who has blown his life and wants to warn others of the mistakes he has made.

I don't like the old stuff, not the classical past, the kings and queens, and the rich and thick, the people who interbred and believed they were chosen by God. They bore me, like they bore most. Endless names on a march to the present during which they do nothing but wallow in their false superiority. But I like the events, the battles, the Romans and the wars. I like the old that I see here. A school based in some type of respectable venture that has turned into a huge factory of kids being groomed to take their pre-defined place in the town. Some will escape, as some always do. But most will stay close and be who they are supposed to be. I don't know what that means for me. I'm not a Greegan, and the Taylor in me is not who I am.

I've looked through and read parts of the book before, sitting here, waiting and reading and getting lost in words and pictures. Such a weird story, such a weird idea full of weird people doing weird things that often flood into the realms of the evil.

A map in 1850, and the centre of a continent is unknown and labelled, here be dragons. That is the weirdest thing. No one knew, no one had been, and no one could ever get there. Now everything is known, everything seen, everything described and understood. A theory for everything, an understanding of action, thought and word. There are many for me and too many for them. We understand, they say. We understand you. But they don't, no matter what they tell me, no matter what I hear. They know nothing, matching me up with a case study carried out on a boy from a bigger country with a different culture and a larger problem. This is what we did to help him, so we will do the same to help you. But they don't help, they tell, and set rules and if I question or ignore then I am failing myself.

Everything repeats but nothing is the same.

Hutton opens the door, smiles at his secretary and motions me in.

9.05 a.m.

His office is light, windows large with nothing covering. A pull-down blind sits compact at the top. His desk is old but kept like new and covered in a shine and polish. The chairs stand out as they are new and chrome-framed with blue covers. The way of it is I sit down and listen. He sits on the edge of his desk, one foot on the ground, like a pool player looking for leverage.

"Was it necessary?" he asks me.

"Being late? Or the swearing?"

"Either?"

"Both."

He pushes up the glasses from his nose and rubs both eyes, one with a thumb and the other with his index finger.

"Tough morning?" he asks.

"Better than some, worse than most," I say.

We wait while he looks at me and I at him, nothing aggressive, but not smiling.

"The world can be awful," he tells me, but I know this. "There are a lot of things we can do to stop it all becoming too much."

"None seem to work."

"What ones are you trying?"

"The ones that help me survive."

"Bad?" he asks.

I nod.

"Want to tell me how?"

I shake my head.

He gives me that look, a look not many throw my way. At least that is how I read it. A look to say he feels my pain, that he understands, but like me there is nothing he can do but just watch and see where it all goes.

"Do you believe things can change?" he asks.

"I don't believe in anything."

"I do."

I look around his office, at the pictures on his shelf, the ornaments he chooses to decorate his space. There is a theme, one of belief.

"You would. You are religious," I tell him.

"That doesn't automatically make me a bad person."

"Doesn't automatically make you a good one either."

He nods because that is the truth and he would never deny that.

"I'm not going to tell you that you are special, not in the sense you have more than others, but I am saying you are worth something. You have a value, something others don't get to decide unless you let them. Unless you agree," he says.

"That's just words. I have what I have, which isn't anything at all."

"There are ways out."

"Not for me there aren't."

"You are wrong about that."

"Seems I can't be right about anything."

He looks at me and smiles like I've walked into a word trap.

"Only a smart kid would say that," he says.

"Maybe only someone dumb would see anything in it."

He taps the table top. The word games he plays, the ones he usually wins have a flaw in logic with me.

"Are you going to run?" he asks, not meaning from life, although there is that. He means from school, which I have done many times before.

"There was that possibility."

He looks at my PE kit.

"First lesson?"

I nod

"How do you fancy isolation for the morning? Sit, read your book?" he asks.

"Your book," I tell him.

Again he pauses and nods and a small smile plays out.

"Read my book. Relax, see where we are at later? No pressure, no work, just sat nice and quiet. I'll have a word. Some thinking time. Not a punishment, although Mr. Crane might believe it to be."

"No PE?"

"You won't even have to break a sweat."

9.15 a.m.

The isolation room looks like an open-plan office. A room in the old buildings that sit around a courtyard. No one likes teaching down here as it is as ancient as it looks. The room is in the corner, the floor wood, parquet I think is the word, but rain has been in, or a flood, or something, because it is buckled and lumped, and smells of aged mould. Tables around the edges, white chipboard panels between each one. Hutton walks me in, the windows painted white so the lights are always on and no one can look in or see out. I've been here before. There is a teacher, although she isn't. There is a woman, Mrs. Brooke, a big lady with a smile and no desire to dye her grey hair. She is probably forty, and she looks like she'd be capable of surviving a prison riot. Her job is to sit and watch the kids sent here to pass time in punishment. But it isn't punishment, not really, just a holding pen for those who teachers don't want around. Occasionally a normal kid will be sent down here, and they will be embarrassed, and feel scared and humiliated and do all they can to never come back, and I guess that is what it is for, that's for who it works. But mostly it is for kids who like it, and don't mind being here, and don't do the work so get to come back again and again. Like the institutionalised incarcerated, they don't have the skills to operate in the mainstream. Here is safe.

For me, here is quiet.

"Morning Ben," Mrs. Brooke says. "How long for?" she asks Mr. Hutton.

He looks at me. "First two lessons," he says. "I'll pop by after, check to see where we are at. He has work from me, no need to chase any up."

He looks to me and nods, the smile gone, the serious face he carries all day set and back where it remains. He turns and with that he is gone.

Mrs. Brooke likes silence more than me. She likes books too, and she reads what seems a novel a day. She would be a librarian but that would mean more work than here.

I open and start to read my own, looking into a three-sided cubicle. There are doodles and words, and shapes etched into the table's surface. A few attempts at carving out designs but they all fall short of complete. The tables have been here as long as the floor, and somebody, somewhere would pay thousands to have them in a restaurant of alternative cool. Eating French aperitifs while reading the biro design saying Jimmy loves Tracey next to a crude outline of a naked lady with unfathomably large breasts. Some hippies would go crazy for that. Maybe the petty thieves should stop aiming for the lead roofing and load up their rusting white vans with generations of old furniture and stools.

The quiet is beautiful and the words I read a way to be away from here and in the past.

I like it there, where I have never been and can never go. Enough of an image to provide the background, and enough blanks in the scene for me to place people and words and thoughts and ideas that would fit, but can never be true.

Maybe I should be less obsessed with what has been and more concerned with what is to come.

Mrs. Brooke doesn't speak, she turns page after page, and that is the only way I know she is there, a sound of paper scraping together, sometimes the small noise made by her licking her index finger. There are buzzes, and the sound of footsteps, but the room is here because of its distance from playgrounds and commotion. The loudest noise will be the bell, or the buzzer, sounding starts and ends. There is a clock in the room, and its tick is rhythmic, but it is not in my view, nothing is beyond a table, three white walls and a book of words. Everything else I see, is from inside my head.

I think of my town, a nothing place of no importance, no industry, no business beyond fish. And I think of the war and the bombs that were dropped, the buildings destroyed and the lives that ended because a German plane wanted to empty its load before flying home. The last of the land of the enemy was here.

I see pictures of then, the fashions, the people and the carnage. Rubble and destruction with normal folk in normal clothes looking like they are tidying up after a large town festival. Each of them believing that moving a brick is part of the greater good.

I look at the pictures and try to understand where they are and what there is now. Some are easy as they have not changed. There is a pillbox on the seafront that is now a place to sit and view the sea. Back then, four men in military gear and a gun because an invasion was possible. The gun no deterrent but there all the same. Maybe it made people feel safe, but looking at it in black and white makes me think it would make me feel scared.

I've seen others, photographic histories of the town, the fifties and sixties, and older still. The main road when it was a lane, the port when it was a pontoon, the pier when it was popular, and the houses that were hotels.

A town with a history, and some remains while most is lost. A photo of the staff of a factory on a day trip. People who were known but are now forgotten, but for the vague memory of an aunt or uncle or grandmother or friend of a friend is all that is left of the people who were the place.

Everything changes and moves on.

The door opens and she walks in. Red hair, but not in the sense of natural, red as in red. Bright red, a shiny, obvious, radiating red covering her long straight hair all the way down her back. I remember her, but not her name. I had no idea she was still at the school.

"Sarah," Mrs. Brooke says. "No need to make the dramatic entrance every day. Take a seat."

She says this while looking up over her book, her annoyance not with the noise or the student, but with the interruption. She plays it cool, and maybe she is. Maybe she doesn't care and that is why she works where she works.

"Billy," Sarah says pointing at me, and it's nice she knows my name. "Greegan's little brother. Shit."

And that's who I am to many: Greegan's little brother. It's used as an insult, pretty much the word equivalent of someone spitting in my face. But it's cool. She isn't the first and not the last.

"Language," Mrs. Brooke says. "Take your usual seat."

Sarah walks, a bouncing cool, her rucksack over her shoulder. She passes me and leans in.

"I hate your brother," she whispers.

Me too I think but stay silent. It is strange that people think I would defend him.

She sits down.

"I'm not doing any work," she says to the room.

"You never do," Mrs. Brooke replies.

I don't look up, don't stare or watch, but I do think. I remember when she appeared in year ten. A year and a half out from exams, this thin, spindly kid with curly hair and long white socks turned up unannounced out of nowhere. No story, no history, just a new student, and one who looked good.

I don't know when the hair changed, no idea hair could be made to be that red. But here she is, with her cheekbones and blue eyes, and legs that are longer than the first years are tall. I don't look her way, I look at my book but don't read. I look at the cover, read the title again and smile at the author. James Hutton. I believe adults call him Jim, while we call him Sir.

Sarah taps something, probably a pen on the table.

"Sarah," Mrs. Brooke says. "Billy there knows you. I know you. Let's face it, anyone having a look round the school remembers the girl with the bright red hair – that's what you want. But, please, among friends, which we are, can you just accept we are giving you all the attention without demanding it through noise? Please?"

"I can't help it," Sarah says.

"Yes, you can. But you don't want to until you have had enough of us looking at you."

"I don't want people looking at me."

"Which is why you tried to look like a lighthouse. You want people to look."

"Bullshit," Sarah says.

"Can you not seek our attention more quietly please? In fact can you do it silently."

"I'm not doing the work."

"I don't have any for you. Because no one sends it through."

"What do I have to do then?"

"Sit in silence and not annoy me."

Sarah responds and sits back and closes her mouth, her thick lips pouting. But she starts to move, small and then big and her mouth opens again. She managed silence for seven seconds.

"Good book?" Sarah asks her.

"Very."

There is another pause. Five seconds this time.

"Sex scenes?" Sarah asks.

"Was in one, but you have ruined the moment."

I think that these two are either related, friends, or have spent a lot of time together.

"Are many others coming?" I ask, having turned round in my chair.

Mrs. Brooke, inhales, lowers her book and stares at me.

"Billy, just because this ball of red hair speaks too much, and breaks my concentration, doesn't mean you get to speak randomly as well. The pair of you can sit and look at things, and think whatever you want. But silently."

9.30 a.m.

The peace - and it is peace - the quiet, the words, the breathing, the knowledge others are there but not caring I am, is a bliss that comes rarely to me. The room of three people, two reading, and one trying to fight her urge to shout and prance and talk and have noise. Sarah taps, and moves in her chair, but has stopped with the words. She is fighting against the absence of interest, nothing to stimulate so she has to move to burn energy.

But our attention and ears click into action as the shouts drift in, and come closer, the footsteps and the swearing, the voice, the recognisable voice, shouting and demanding to know who is in isolation.

Mrs. Brooke swears, puts down her book. I turn in my chair, stand and my face, I know, losing colour and my eyes growing wide.

The commotion outside, the commotion getting close, doors opened, questions shouted, Iso used as a shorthand for it all, bouncing along, stepping toward me. I hear and I know. I look to

Sarah and her face is panic. The swearing close now, the school aware of the presence, of the anger and of the threat.

"Who's in there? Who is in iso?"

He is coming here because this is the place he will relate to school, will relate to where kids like me and him are found.

Darren opens the door to the isolation room. We see him, or part of him and he sees part of me. Mrs. Brooke blocks the way, standing tall and wide like a doorman at a London venue. The door isn't on any mechanism, just old hinges, thick, screwed in a hundred years ago and hidden under layers of cheap white gloss.

Darren stares at the woman blocking his way, not knowing what to do, not knowing if violence is the way. But knowing her, and knowing what she does.

"Get out of the way," he says, stepping forward.

Mrs. Brooke tenses, becomes bigger, blocks the doorway and doesn't move. Darren stops his charge, the plan had been for her to step aside.

"I don't want to hurt you," Darren says.

"I wasn't banking on you being chivalrous," Mrs. Brooke says. "But I am banking on you being a little wimp. Imagine the embarrassment of being taken down by little old me."

"You aren't little."

"And you aren't fighting."

Darren looks behind him, and I hear feet and voices. Easy to recognise, easy to hear. A group of teachers, mostly from PE.

"I could hurt you," Darren whispers, the way he has threatened me over the years.

"You could try," Mrs. Brooke says, and I fear for her husband.

Darren turns away, the people behind him of more concern than the woman in front.

"The police are coming, Darren," Mr. Crane says, and I catch a glimpse of the little man, standing at the front of four teachers. Two much larger than him, younger too, not yet retired from rugby.

Crane is confident, speaking from distance, far enough to have time to react and run. His back-up is there, his confidence radiating. Darren thinks him small and weak and pathetic, I know this because we all think the same, and I guess Crane knows that himself. He can only delude himself so much. But now, with men behind, his confidence for confrontation has grown.

"What's in the bag?" Hutton asks, his voice soft.

I look and Darren is holding a small sports bag, tightly balled up, held close, as if it contains the secret to life.

"Clothes," Darren tells him.

"The police are on their way, Darren," Hutton says with that hypnotic voice of calm.

Hutton has taken control, stepped through Crane's bluster and noise. He is speaking to reduce tension, to bring nerves down with a voice pitched at soothing. Darren has tuned in.

"I just want to speak to Billy," he says. "That's all."

"Can't let that happen right now," Hutton says. "It is the wrong way to approach it. We can speak, see where we get. But if we stay calm, we can see when we can."

Darren looks left and right, knows there is no one behind him.

"Billy," he shouts, "We need to speak. I need to tell you something."

Sarah is quiet, looking at me, watching to see if I open my mouth. She is scared, and I am too. But I'm not speaking, not to these people. The time will come, tonight I guess. Whatever form that takes will be better than the one right now.

I don't know how I look, I don't know what shows on my face, I don't know if I hide what I am feeling or I am easy to read. I don't have any way of knowing what I let people see. At home it doesn't matter, what I feel, what they see in me is of no concern. They do what they do based on them.

"You okay?" Sarah asks.

I shake my head.

"You ever hated someone?" I ask her.

She stares at me.

"Yeah, a couple," she says. "Darren is one of them."

And there I am, condemned by association to a mad man.

"I don't know what he did to you, but I'm sorry for whatever that might be-"

"Not your apology to make."

"But," I say, not having other words to add. "It doesn't matter."

Whatever I feel, it doesn't matter. There isn't a way out, not yet.

The loud words come from outside.

"You need to back off," Darren shouts.

"Mr. Crane, step away," Hutton says, a snatch and bite to his words. "Darren, whatever it is that has happened, that you may have done, or are thinking of doing, I can help. Mr. Crane stop."

"The game is up," Crane says, stepping forward, not understanding.

Crane is a fool. A real, genuine fool.

"Back off," Darren tells him, but Crane is full of false confidence, reading everything wrong and believing he has power through a job title.

"You need to relax, be quiet and wait," Crane orders. "So just stay there."

Darren tenses, the switch he makes, the change. Crane can't see it, can't understand. He has thrown an insult without knowledge and without the means to protect himself.

"The hell?" Darren says.

I see Hutton look to Crane, anger there in his eyes, but holding on to the calm.

Darren steps forward, reaches out and grabs Crane's collar and tie, bunching up his fist, pulling the cotton tight. He pulls, and Hutton screams "Darren." But there is no point. Darren pulls and drives his head forward and plants his forehead on Crane's nose. There is a crack, as bone collides through a minimal cushion of flesh. Crane drops, Darren lets go. Hutton stares, as do we as the two PE teachers move forward.

Darren swears, bends forward at the waist, screams again. He stands. Looks at everyone, looks at what he has done. He turns and runs with Crane writhing on the floor and Hutton looking on, shaking his head while Mrs. Brooke raises an eyebrow at the little man on the floor and smiles.

9.40 a.m.

"Do you know what that was about?" Hutton asks me.

He and Mrs. Brooke have come back into the room.

I shake my head.

"Something from this morning?" he asks.

I don't know, I don't know anything. I have nothing to say, nothing at all. I need to think, I know that. Darren coming here, for me, to talk, or whatever his intentions were, makes no sense. I doubt they make sense to him. But it is new, nothing that has happened before. The fight this morning, the head shot, maybe it shook him up, maybe it had an effect. I don't know. I don't know anything.

"I don't know what is happening," I tell them.

The police arrive and so does Crane's ambulance. He refuses with blood on his face and shirt. A little tough man fooling no one. But the hospital can't fix his broken pride. Mrs. Brooke, Sarah and me in isolation. A room not taking any more visitors for the time being. Mrs. Brooke reading, but not. Her concentration broken, her ability to pretend not as good as she thinks. Sarah watches me, and I look at the same photo in a history book trying to memorise it all. A church destroyed by a second world war bomb. A woman with a scarf on her head and a thick dressing gown stood on top of bricks and a half-fallen wall as children and men stand in the background watching and looking at the destruction. I've seen it before, but I look for details I missed. There is nothing there.

"Is his nose broken?" Sarah asks.

"Looked that way," Mrs. Brooke replies, not looking up from the page she has been on for more than a minute. "But nothing to do with us. I believe Darren may need a little help."

"He needs a kicking," Sarah tells her.

"Never solved anything."

"I'm not talking about curing, I'm talking about getting even."

"Not our jobs, not our concern, and not something to talk about."

We sit in silence, no pages turning, Sarah fidgeting as a pressure of words builds up inside until she can't contain them anymore.

"He like that at home?" she asks.

"Sarah," Mrs. Brooke says.

"I'd like to know. Living with that, how can you do it? What is that all about? That shouldn't be allowed."

I feel and want to explain, to defend, because if I don't they will think I am the same.

"He isn't like that," I say, almost believing me. "His dad is - worse too. A lot worse. That's all he knows. That's who he is. It's all he has got."

"You aren't like that," Sarah says.

I turn my head to take my stare from the floor to her face.

"If I were bigger and stronger I would be. If I were twice as big, twice as strong, I'd fight too. I'd put him down. I would. But I'm not, so I can't, so I don't."

Mrs. Brooke puts her book down.

"You don't have to explain anything, Billy," she says. "And you need to stop asking questions, little miss nosey. It is none of your, or our, business."

"But people like that, people like Darren running around, doing all that. Hurting people."

"You against Crane having his face flattened now, are you?" Mrs. Brooke asks.

"Well, no. That I can take."

"So it is Okay for people you don't like, but not for the people you actually like? That's not how things work."

"He was asking for it," Sarah says.

"You think Darren has been asking for his life?" I say.

"You get to choose," Sarah tells me.

"Do you? Really?" Mrs. Brooke asks. "Are we all here and who we are through our own choices? You think that? Believe that?"

"What do you think?" Sarah asks, a touch of scorn because someone disagrees.

"I think you need to read more. I think you need to live more, and I think you need to understand more before judging and condemning people based on some set of rules you, as a fifteen-year old girl, have created to understand the world you live in. That's what I think. But I also think we all need to be quiet and just let the events sink in. That is definitely what is best."

9.55 a.m.

Hutton comes and gets me and I know why, I know who is here. An hour of isolation.

"Darren had a mark on his face," Hutton says as we walk from isolation to his office.

"I didn't see," I tell him and that is the truth.

"Anything to do with this morning?"

"Nothing to do with me, no," I say.

"Not quite what I asked."

"I didn't see it so I couldn't describe it."

We walk a few steps and Hutton sighs.

"Okay, Billy," he says. "I understand."

But he doesn't, he is just trying, forcing his ideas, principles and beliefs to bend so the anger he feels doesn't overwhelm. I guess that is a trick to becoming calm.

"Is it uniform or plain clothes?" I ask.

"What do you mean?"

"The police you are taking me to see, are they in blue or normal clothes."

He inhales again, like a kind man told he needs to wait another hour after being stood all day.

"Uniform," he tells me.

This is a good thing, plain clothes is proper trouble. The squad cars are for turning up and people seeing and the school knowing that behaviour gets punished. It isn't something to brush discreetly.

"Any reason they want to talk to me?"

"I have no doubt you know more than me," Hutton says. "Your brother being here isn't all of it, and the part before I could only guess at. You, however, will know."

We walk the rest of the way in silence, a minute at most, until we are in his secretary's office and his door is open.

"You aren't one of them, Billy. And you don't have to be. Be you," he says as a policeman waves me in.

10.00 a.m.

I sit where Hutton has me sit whenever I have to visit, and there are two officers, both large, although it is difficult to tell with all the layers they have on, if they are natural or padded. They wait, like they always do to add pressure or see if I will start talking or just because they think they can make me feel uncomfortable. I don't, I can't understand why I would be.

"Seen your brother?" the one on the left asks.

They are, if I squint, like a modern set of twins.

"Earlier and every day," I say.

I know my tone, I know my contempt, and I know this is because I have been told and taught that the way to communicate with these people is through being difficult and treating them as stupid. But honestly, I have been taught not to trust anyone, not just these. But these more than anyone else.

"Are you just another on the production line?" policeman two asks, and he has got there too quickly, too soon to try the bully.

"I'm nobody," I say.

"You owe him nothing," number one tells me.

"Even less than that."

"He doesn't care about you," number two adds.

"And me him."

"But you'll lie for him."

"Where have I lied?"

"Holding back information is the same," number one tells me.

"You haven't asked any questions."

They look at each other, something that means they need to agree. They don't want me to hear the words.

"Do you think your brother could hurt someone?" Number one asks.

"Seems you guys do."

"Why would you say that?"

"Because of the question you asked."

"So do you?"

"What?"

"Think he could hurt someone?"

"All people can. Most things can if you give them a reason. Pretty sure a toddler could if they were strong enough."

"Was he here to hurt you?" Number ones asks, and it seems number two is now only a witness.

"Didn't seem that way? But I never got to ask."

"Has he ever hurt you?"

"Two boys in a house? Of course he has."

"Why did he do that?"

"Because he is stronger than me."

"Why did you fight?"

"To see who goes where in the order of things."

"And where are you?"

"At the bottom. Just above you guys."

Number two flinches at this but he holds his peace.

"So no idea the reason he was here," Number one asks. "Nor any insight in to what it might have been?"

"You'd need to ask him."

They look at each other again. Number two can't hold it anymore.

"He isn't escaping," he tells me.

"And it doesn't sound like you need my help. But good luck."

They know, they have seen the like of me before. They know I won't talk, and they know they don't have time to try tricks and repetitions until I make a mistake and they jump in. They need my help but they don't need me to admit guilt. I have done nothing wrong and they have nothing to create a bond. They aren't my friends, they don't like me, they don't care and anything they say is simply a means to get what they want.

I don't like Darren, I can't say I hate, that is too strong, too powerful an emotion. I don't care what happens as that is on him. His decisions and his actions and they consequences are there to see. But the outcome is a caution, a telling off and continued freedom. If I speak, Darren will know and the only one who is punished is me. The logic of what they are asking is a collapse in my well-being. They fake a bond to elicit my help in the knowledge that it would be an act of self-harm. I am not dumb enough to go for it.

"Is this what you want?" Number two asks me.

"Which is what?" I ask, hoping for the time we have left to be taken up with a speech from a man who is no better than me about how the world works in his own mind.

"To be like this? To be someone who helps people like Darren, who helps people destroy what's around them."

"Be more you?"

They smile at me, condescending and arrogant because that's what they have. And that, to them is all I am.

10.10 a.m.

"Did you tell them anything?" Hutton asks me.

The police left, I stayed sat and Hutton came in. All an easy flow of events and the order of things.

"I had nothing to say."

"There is a difference between having nothing and saying nothing, you understand that."

I shrug and Hutton smiles.

"You have more than you know, that's something you don't understand."

"Just trying to survive," I say, smiling.

"Want to head back to isolation or lessons?"

There is no need to think. Back into the crowds or the easy space of isolation.

"I'm going to go with isolation."

"Want to be alone or like the company."

"Mrs. Brooke rarely speaks."

"Very good, Billy. Very good," Mr. Hutton says.

We walk, slowly, more than when we came to his office. The noise is low, kids in classrooms, some listening, most not.

"You going to be ok?" Hutton asks.

"In what sense? Like forever?"

"Tonight. Going home?"

"Sir, I don't know what is happening. There was a fallout, nothing strange there. Darren came off worse, but soon he won't. Quinn made sure he let me know I shouldn't try the same. I don't know why Darren was here, I don't really care right now. When I see him, I'll know. I'll try not to see him until I can. People have it worse."

"That doesn't mean you have to accept what you have."

"Just makes me feel better is all."

We keep on walking and the wall around the school has trees that are older than the buildings, and bigger than them too. I don't know what they are, I could ask but it is better to wonder sometimes. I don't need to know and sometime in the future the information will be revealed and I'll think that those old ones now have a name. Or maybe I'll never find out and that will mean I just don't care. I'll hold the image though, make sure I can match them up if the time is right.

"Is there a lot of violence at home?" Hutton asks.

I snort, not because this is natural but because it seems the only way to answer stupidity.

"You taught Darren and you know Quinn, I'm sure you'd have heard of him too. So what do you think?"

"I think I want to hear you."

"Not happening."

We walk and I don't know why, possibly the extended silence, possibly I just want to know if he bothered to find out.

"Do you know what those trees are?"

I point at the biggest, the one that stands out as the oldest and strongest, with its rough bark and huge branches and large green leaves. It doesn't produce conkers, or anything other than a sap and seeds. They are everywhere in town, a lot of houses with one on the boundary between garden and street. They are everywhere.

"I don't," Hutton says. "Why?"

"I see them every day, could tell if one was gone, but I never bothered to find out anything about them. Seemed pointless. Why would I need to know?"

Hutton stops walking and turns to me and looks down.

"If you put your mind to something, you'd have a chance to achieve it."

"I put my mind to a lot of things, and I'm not dead yet," I tell him.

10.20 a.m.

The isolation room is as I left. Mrs. Brooke sat reading, Sarah is sat fidgeting and she smiles when she sees me. Hutton tells

Mrs. Brooke that I am there for the day. My bag and book are where I left them.

"All ok?" Mrs. Brooke asks me when she is sure Hutton has gone.

"All good. Not sure what they wanted."

"Now I imagine that isn't true. You might not know exactly, you might not know details, but you'll have a good enough idea. But I don't need to know. I just need the quiet. Missy here, however, needs the noise."

We look at Sarah, and her mouth is open, ready and loaded with whatever her brain is thinking at a million miles an hour. But she somehow stops, and smiles, and turns her back to her small space of white isolation.

"At a girl," Mrs. Brooke says.

The silence, or near as to it that it makes no difference drags out and hits a rhythm of peace. I flick through pages, reading paragraphs and I think I have made the leap from the panic of the present, in the here and now, to the confused peace of the past where my imagination combines with the written facts to create stories and feelings for the world as it was. The clean polite history of war. A time when everyone is depicted as heroes, at least those on the side that won, and there are no villains. The bad people, they have all, in written form, become good. Every last one. The old days where people were better. But it can't be true. There must have been evil, must have been those who I see now, those with vanity, those with aggression, those backed up in action by their own stupidity and arrogance. But it isn't here on the page, it isn't written. Here is just how everyone came together, everyone, despite what they may have been, united as one and each became a better part of the whole. I don't believe this is real. If there were a war now would Quinn and Darren and Crane all become better people? Would the threat of death from a bomb on their home make who they are change into something they are not? I can't believe it. I could hope, I could possibly fool myself into believing in a moment of need they would stand up and be real, honest people fighting to protect us all. But I know them, I live with them, they are actors in my life, actors in how I am and will be, and I can't trick myself into buying the idea they are, in different circumstances, people to trust, respect and cherish. A photograph now, of them, and me, seen in fifty years' time would show whatever the person looking wanted to see. Three males, in a photo with a story, or multiple stories to be told in the minds of those who see it. And none of them would be true. None of them would tell of the fear. We would look like a family, a group who are showing their bonds through posing for posterity. Nothing is true, nothing that can be seen in a snapshot.

The bell rings and Sarah, who it seems has been testing herself, lets out a "Thank Fuck."

"Congratulations," Mrs. Brooke says. "The longest you have been quiet while not asleep."

"Told you I could do it."

"No, you didn't. You just did it. But again, congratulations. I'm impressed, and dare I say it, emotional. That is some willpower."

I smile, looking at the pair of them, the bond they seem to have.

"Any plans on trying to smash that time this afternoon, tomorrow and on all the other days you will be here until your hair changes colour?"

Sarah smiles at this like a small demon ready to possess a soul.

"Is that really the reason you are here? Red hair?" I ask.

Sarah nods.

"It is," she says. "Apparently this makes me evil and not worth educating. Apparently, the rules say unnatural colour hair is banned. It doesn't say why, or explain how it affects my ability to learn, or the negative effect it has on those close-by, but it is banned all the same."

"Those are the rules," Mrs. Brooke says, simultaneously explaining and not explaining.

"Rules which make no sense," Sarah tells her.

"Got to wear a uniform too," Mrs. Brooke says.

"Why?" Sarah asks.

"So as not to discriminate."

Sarah turns and pints at me.

"Look at Billy. Look at his uniform. It's clearly a mess – sorry Billy, but it is – and he'll get bullied for it. Does it improve his life? No."

"Better than wearing the same clothes every day," I say.

"You do. That is the uniform."

"But if I wore what I wanted, I wouldn't have much of a selection. So I'd get hassle all the same."

Sarah stares at me, and shakes her head, after the briefest of pauses to try and understand what I have just said.

"Whatever. The rules make no sense. Blazers on until it reaches a temperature the head teacher finds uncomfortable. Then, on his word, we can walk round in shirts, but only if the shirt has a badge. No badge, blazer on. Total madness."

"So you break all the rules and come here day after day to what? Prove a point?" Mrs. Brooke asks.

"Maybe."

"Maybe. Or maybe you are just a bit scared of being in with the others and finding out stuff, and being someone normal."

"I don't aim to be normal."

"You aren't."

"Thanks."

"In a good way."

12.25 p.m.

We get to pass through the queue at the canteen. Being in isolation means we must be isolated. We don't get to stand and wait with kids at school, we get to go through. Sarah gets catcalls, and why not? Bright red hair and long legs are something for boys to cheer and demean with ways they have learned from their fathers and each other. Sarah smiles and tells a few where to go but she doesn't seem annoyed, certainly not angry, almost buzzing that she gets to ridicule in return.

"That bother you?" I ask when we have walked along the queue of hundreds to the place where we choose what we want from the limited selection of poorly cooked, and poorly looked after food. A massive hotplate of carbohydrates in the form of chips and other potato products. Everything too hot and already dry. I take the chips and the sausages and add gravy. Sarah takes the same.

"Why would it bother me?" she says, holding her tray. "They are idiots and I am not."

"But all the hassle and attention."

"Standard. Not like they are ever going to be a friend or someone I'll speak to."

"All the time?"

"Like I said, standard. What can I do? So I just sneer because that is all they're worth."

"I couldn't handle it."

"You'll never have to."

We sit down at a table in the corner, the canteen filling up from the other end. We are the iso kids on the iso table and we are left alone but people stare. I start to eat and while I know it is poor quality and cooked in some massive container that probably hasn't been cleaned in three academic years, the gravy is good and thick and makes everything ok.

"You hungry?" Sarah asks.

I look up, chips chewing in my mouth, and half a sausage about to join it.

"Slow down," she says. "You finish, you have to go back."

I look up and stare.

"I like it there," I say.

"You won't with indigestion."

I stare at her some more smiling at the stupidity of concern.

"I sound like your mum, right?" she says, smiling too.

I shake my head as I chew.

"You aren't shouting and you aren't slurring your words, so not really, no," I tell her.

Her smile tries to stay on her face and something similar is vaguely there, but the sad smile, the concerned smile that I get and hate and try to turn into a snarl as soon as I can appears on her lips.

"Bad?" she asks.

I shrug holding a fork.

"Just who she is, with me at least."

"She the same with Darren?"

"Not her son, so no. Quinn's job is Darren."

We eat some more, Sarah slowly and me barely breaking the stuff down into chunks I can swallow. Sarah eats most of it and puts down her fork.

"What was it with Darren this morning?"

Everybody wants to know. I put down the cutlery too.

"Had a fight with Quinn. Lost. Bit closer than previous times. Still lost though. It's as if he won't do it unless it is a fair fight. Quinn all ready to go, at the top of his game. He won't do it when Quinn is drunk, or passed out, or whatever. Needs to beat the man."

"What has that got to do with you?"

"Nothing. I'm missing something. Probably something that doesn't actually exist or something that hasn't actually happened, but it is my fault all the same. Probably turned up to give me a slap along with the blame."

"He sounded pretty gone."

"He sounded out of his mind. And that is some way to go because he isn't all there to start with."

She is staring at me now, and I can't understand why, can't read the thought or what she is feeling. Curious is all I see.

"What?" I ask.

"Nothing," she tells me.

12.45 p.m.

I can feel them looking, most eyes in the canteen. The place fills quickly because we have fifty minutes and as few of them on eating is the best way to go. There are places to hang out, people to see and walks to be had in the break between lessons. Stuffing stodgy food down your throat is the least of most kids priorities. But I hear the name Darren said again and again. I see and feel the points. It is all normal, all the same just exaggerated today. No idea what that idiot was thinking. He had been to this school, done his time as he would say, and left with nothing. A few letters way down the alphabet to tell anyone who asked, and no one ever will, what his level of ability on a random subject is best represented with a grade. He was always going to work with his hands on sites where others have skill and he has to pick stuff up. He has nothing but the body of a young man who will try and get bigger. His whole life here was a waste of his and their time, and probably had a serious impact on some kids around him. Imagine being told to sit next to that freak in a lesson. What are you going to do?

He had his kickings because he'd fight anyone. The older boys when Darren was young were happy to slap him about, chuck him in hedges and down ditches. The kid couldn't shut up or back off. But he got older and there were no bigger kids. Everyone else had moved on from fighting, but he hadn't, and he didn't mind slapping the little ones. The bigger lads handed him a beating when he went too far.

Everyone expects the same of me. My name associated with him and all his glory.

But this is another level. I am centre of attention. Some wild-eyed idiot that some remember and most have heard stories about, came into school, dropped Crane and ran. The only connection they have between that and them is me. For whatever reason they think I am a celebrity to scorn for the day. Words and Darrens and points and my own name thrown into the mix. It is like everyday here just multiplied by large numbers I don't know how to name. A million doesn't sound enough.

"Let's go," Mrs. Brooke says.

She had sat at a distance, giving us space, or her the time away she wants. I don't know. She is cool, but maybe that is just one way of interpreting the idea she doesn't really care because caring causes stress and she wants none of that. I don't know. It is cynical, really genuinely cynical, but it is a way of being I have constructed to help me defend myself against the lies and tricks and games of everyone I meet.

"You okay?" Sarah asks as we stand.

I shrug, my universal reply to the world. It can mean whatever you want because to me it means nothing at all.

We have to walk back through the crowd because the logical way out is blocked. There is the need to turn the whole routine into a one-way system, but that way would take us out into a playground, and require a walk around buildings, up stairs and back into the courtyard where the isolation building stands. We walk and kids turn and stare because they are in groups and outnumber me, and they are all buzzing on gossip, some of which will be descriptions of what they have seen, mostly of lies they have heard, probably from kids who make stuff up on a regular to try and calm their imaginative minds.

The place is heaving, the corridor for the queue a mass of uniforms, in groups, not lined up but all knowing where they stand. There are no teachers because it is impossible to manage. The tables are full, and people are sat in their groups, with their friends, and they are all talking and the noise is a continual pop of words. When a choir joins up and their combined voice hits the note required despite many being out of tune. The conversation sounds like the population talking in unison about a topic they agreed on during maths hour. Occasionally there are shouts but it isn't from violence, or scares or assault, it is from jokers whose punchlines are loud screams to scare those who don't see it coming. One is the kids who can't just be one of the crowd and have to be the one in the middle, the one who has to have all eyes, or at least all those around them, staring at their magnificence.

The hall is big when empty, but cramped now, the tall windows open, the doors never closed, a breeze running through carrying the noise. I feel it though, the eyes and the points, and the stares and the laughter. Billy Greegan, brother of Darren, the mad bastard that came in and nutted Crane. The kid who looks unwashed and uncared for, one of the scum, one of the bums who will leave here with no future and no friends and nothing but the company of Darren to get him through the days. They know they can take me, they know my history isn't of violence, but a history of hiding, a history of corners. There is no kickback from me, no punches thrown, no vengeance sought until paid back in pain. I threaten no one, I cause no one to fear me. They know Darren wouldn't defend me, although the possibility is enough to deter most. But me, here, alone, and the police after my step-brother, leaves me vulnerable and them filled with confidence. I am part of the story for them, despite the real plot being me as a character there to flesh out space. I'm not even a paragraph in their novel. Not something that even needs a description. I'm an unknown boy in a photo in a history book. Young, scruffy kid in school, undated and unnamed. I don't belong here, and in the future when people look back and talk of the fun of school, I will be someone they don't remember. I'll make sure I don't forget them.

We push through and groups turn and watch as they would anyone walking against the grain. There should be a space but there isn't, and the shiny brick of the inside are rubbed smoother with shoulders and backs and bags and arms as kids jostle for space and position. They move for Mrs. Brooke, but I get the feel that adults move for her. The ones that haven't seen, the ones taken up in their scuffles and flirts are the ones to look now, the ones to look at me from my head down to my shoes and then back. I am evaluated and rated and categorized in the briefest moment, the shortest assumption on how I appear. The end point is always the same, always the conclusion. They smile, laugh or reel in horror at me, the unclean and uncool. Sarah's presence is taking none of the heat, she has faded, just someone else who is near to the boy no one likes because of other people, people they think I love.

Some, the older ones, will remember Darren, and some, without doubt will have been his victims in some way at some point. They can't even that out, but they can hope the police put it all straight, and they will have me as the same, as the one who backed him up by living in the same house and having to carry the same name.

I don't like the feeling, the burden or weight or both of someone else's troubles. I have caused little. I have stayed quiet when asked to speak, I have spoken when silence was demanded. I have never caused destruction or hurt to those who didn't come at me first. I don't talk, don't engage and don't really know how to talk to the kids in my school. I did once, when I was little, I spoke all the time, chatting away in primary school, playing on pedal cars and with water and sand in a playground while women with big hair and bright clothes and chatty nature watched and made sure we didn't get hurt. I remember running, laughing, playing and having friends, people who came to me, kids who thought I was fun. But it faded to nothing, and I caused that too. I was involved, not all, not all on me. Like now, with these people I don't know, whose names I know from a register repeated day after day. I know them in alphabetical order. But I don't speak because they don't want me to speak. I don't come in enough for them to hear me. I sit alone and listen mostly.

I came in today to avoid home, to avoid being alone, to avoid walking and sitting and looking at nothing, trying to stay away from people in the woods and the fields around the town. But I came in and it is that way, the same. I am alone but the object of everyone's eyes and words. And that is worse. They see me but don't know me. I am the scorn they feel for another in feeble body and dirty clothes and someone they know can be the one to call names and insult without any comeback. Why would I shout? Why would I try and take on so many with my single voice? I could do nothing but make it worse.

I feel the panic come on, my heart flutter and kick into a thump. I am prickly, my skin wet, the noise and sounds and the light I see all becoming too much too quickly. I can hear everything but nothing I want. The movement makes me sick, the people never still, the kids all pushing and walking and marching, an overload. I can do this with ease but they are looking and talking as if they know, but they don't. They have judged and decided a long time ago and today, with Darren, has given them all the evidence they need even though I am not involved. Guilty by association.

"Come on, Billy," Sarah says, and she pushes me lightly in my back.

I step forward and the noise is there, the chatter and voices. I see Mrs. Brooke ahead and people moving out of the way, kids sense her, turn and step aside. Like cars speeding behind an ambulance, we try and keep up and walk in the space she leaves behind before the wall of uniforms seeps in and fills the gap.

"You okay?" Sarah asks.

"You keep asking that."

"Waiting for you to answer with the truth."

"I'm good."

"No, you aren't. You are clammy and shaking."

I look at my hands as we walk and see the quivers, the same as Quinn's but not as bad as his mornings. The shakes and the trembles, the jokes and the sighs. It is the wound of a life well lived, he thinks, but to others it is the sign of a man addicted.

13.00 p.m.

It was a mistake to come in, I should have wandered the town and country and just wallowed like a child in the misery I decide to bathe in. It is all stupid, none of it with sense and none of it worth the time. There is nothing happening, nothing to gain, no positive to have from being here. Sarah is walking next to me, my shoulders are slumped and Mrs. Brooke is steps away from the door to isolation.

"How fast are you?" Sarah asks.

"Slow. Really slow."

"Can you run?"

"Probably, been a while."

I try to think of the last time that I ran, properly sprinted, and I think it was primary school where the top boy was whoever was quickest. The way to the summit was through speed decided through races. I ran and I never won. But I joined in and tried, always thinking I could win, maybe that one time.

"Want to have fun?" Sarah asks, her face lit up and her eyes bigger.

"In what way?"

She stares at me for the briefest of moments, looking into my face, searching for something.

"Yeah, you do. I see that," she says and smiles and I have no idea what she thinks.

"Don't go in," she says.

She starts to speed up and I don't keep pace, she breaks into a half-jog, and passes Mrs. Brooke. Sarah pushes the door, goes in and Mrs. Brooke looks back at me. I can tell her nothing beyond confusion with my expression. I know nothing.

As Mrs. Brooke turns back, Sarah flies out of the door carrying her bag and mine. She is running.

"Sarah," Mrs. Brooke shouts.

"Sorry," Sarah shouts back.

"Don't do it," Mrs. Brooke shouts again, but Sarah is motoring at speed, running at me, she throws my bag and I catch it.

"Let's go, slow boy," she says, slowing but not stopping.

She sprints off, heading for the gate at the bottom of the playground. Mrs. Brooke watches her, but turns to look at me. She shakes her head. I look around, school kids watching, the attention zooming in. The same kids who stare with scorn and talk openly about me as someone not to be near. They are all watching.

"Be smart Billy," Mrs. Brooke says.

"Come on," Sarah shouts.

Mrs. Brooke raises a walkie-talkie to her mouth and I hear the crackle as she presses the button to speak.

"Come on," Sarah shouts again.

I look around, see all those kids, all those faces and all those people who have never said a word to me. I scan them all, looking for anything to tell me to stay.

I mouth a swear word, turn to Sarah and run. I hear her laugh and I hear her feet on the ground as she sprints too, and I see her hair flowing back as we run for the open gate past students who have made the decision to leave the site.

She runs and I try to catch up but I can't. I stay in touch and see where she goes. We sprint down the hill, across the playground, out of the gate, weaving through a few students too lazy to go fast or too bored to move at speed. We are out into the street and houses, a small lane leading down to the ring road, houses on each side and a Methodist church of bland grey at the bottom and on the left. There is a walkway around its wall, a high wall on one side protecting the land inside and a hedge on the other protecting the gardens of large terraced houses. She runs and I follow and I hope she stops or slows. My breathing hard and my legs tired after only seconds of sprinting. She gets to the end of the lane, looks left and right on a small road with double-yellows on either side, jogs across, steps into a lane that runs behind a row of small cottages. She stops and looks back, bending forward, her hands on her knees and her bag falling down off her shoulder, catching her on her neck.

I amble across the road not to be cool but because my muscles are on fire and my lungs are burning.

Sarah is giggling.

"What's the plan?" I ask.

She looks up, gasping for air.

"Plan? Are you mental? That was the plan. What happens next is up to us. A plan? Jesus, Billy."

She laughs and starts to stand.

"But getting far away is best. They can only really chase so far."

"I'm not running."

"I'm not asking you to, but be discreet."

We walk to the end of the lane where it drops down via cracked paving slab steps where weeds have come through. The steps are opposite a pub, a pub with toilets upstairs and old men prefer the walk across the road to here to urinate and the smell lingers.

"Be careful," Sarah says. "Hold your breath."

It is like the phonebox up on the estates, the red cabin with no glass and a floor of cigarette butts and damp. That overpowering smell left behind by people making calls on public phones and talking into a mouthpiece that has been breathed on by hundreds, and used as a toilet by a few. Sarah jumps down the last step like a primary school kid setting themselves a little dare and we are on the edge of the town centre, behind the local supermarket, near bins, and the backdoor of a pub that is popular because it is cheap and near the taxi rank. It has a sun garden, which is no sun trap just a dark hedged-in area for the kids to play in while mothers and fathers drink the afternoon away. I never came here as a kid, nor now as a teen, the prices not cheap enough for a family day out of drinking.

    We edge around the town and there are school kids in their uniforms drifting about, killing time and messing around. They pay little to no attention to us, the word isn't out and those that leave the site are those who don't care mostly. And there aren't enough of them, not in the small groups, to shout and cause trouble. There is always a space between us.

    The sea front pops up quickly, the promenade running all the way along from the mouth of the river to the rocks, two miles away where the only way to pass is by boat or through a train tunnel. Walking means going all the way around. The seawall has a path that runs all the way, at the foot of a cliff. There is a second road, a small one-way lane that pushes up the hill, winding along its edge next to fields and a park for walking dogs. We take this and I realise we are not speaking.

    "Why did you run?" I ask.

"Same reason you followed," she tells me.

"I don't know why."

"There we go."

I think about this as we walk the ever increasingly steep lane with small green areas to our right and a large park to our left. I don't know why I ran. I knew I wanted out, knew I felt discomfort and anxiety about the attention, the noise and the people. Knew I need to hide away. Isolation would have done that for me, Mrs. Brooke silent turning pages. Sarah would have spoken, no way she can do more time not talking. But Sarah ran, she decided for me. She threw my bag and I turned and chased. Going back isn't an option. The embarrassment of when I go back in a certain.

The path has turned from tarmac to gravel and there is a hinged gate we pass through, something to stop wild animals marching down. The other side is more lane, but short now as there is a large road ahead, one at the top of the valley overlooking the river and the sea. A house made expensive because it has large windows. We stand at the top, the peak of the town and look around us, spinning and taking it all in.

"Know anyone who lives up here?" Sarah asks.

"I don't know anyone who lives on my street, not anyone I'd want to remember. You?"

"Not one."

We stand and look around at the trees that line the lane we walked, the houses with their big gates and high walls. Someone sometime built a big protective barrier around what are little more than old cottages. The air is good up here, not that air is bad, it just feels fresh and clean.

13.30 p.m.

We sit a few metres from the edge of the cliff, the wind blowing strong and the view out onto choppy sea. The land swings down to the right, flowing into the town and its cramped houses and outdated streets.

"Weird being here," Sarah says.

"In a field?"

"In this town. It isn't mine. A couple of years ago I wouldn't have been able to tell you where it was."

"I think a lot of people spend a lot of time trying to forget."

She looks at me and pouts her lips not to be sexy but to exaggerate the confused.

"You say some deep stuff for someone who-"

"Is thick?"

"Yeah. A lot of sense for one of the school tards."

"Thanks."

We sit and watch the water and feel the wind, and we are leaning back on our hands as if watching a free show in a park. It feels like an hour but is probably only minutes.

"Why did you come to this place, of all the places you could go. Why would anyone choose here?" I ask.

She turns to me, confusion reigning her face.

"I didn't choose," she says. "I got sent. Or selected. Or someone chose me. Or something. I don't know. It is as good a place as any to hide."

I look at her, reeled in by the vague hints, the words used to elicit a response. It isn't the first time she has used them, I know that, I'm not dumb.

"You don't know?" she asks.

"Don't know what?"

"Don't know me."

"I found out your name today. I remember you turning up."

"Looked different then, didn't I?"

"You looked good."

"Not now?"

"Now too."

She laughs at this.

"Always the right answer. Get a lot of practice?"

"I don't speak much."

"I think you have a lot to say."

"Nothing happy."

We sit and listen as sea birds talk or warn or fight. The noises always high-pitched and annoying.

"Do you like Hutton?" she asks.

I think about this, not because I am unsure of the answer, but because I am unsure of how much to say. But I'm not lying, not about him.

"I do, yeah. I know he is a teacher and all that. And religious, to a degree. But he is good, I like him. He has never done anything bad, never spoken to me like I'm an idiot."

She watches me as I say this, looking at my mouth as I form words and care.

"Do you not?" I ask.

She pauses to think, trying not to hurt my feelings, not to disagree and fall out. It isn't like she has anyone else to talk to.

"I'd really like not to."

Despite myself I can't hide the surprise, my face telling a story of disappointment. She grins at this, my pain at the insults aimed at a man I shouldn't like.

"I live with him," she says.

I know what this means. I understand. I think my mouth opens. I get what she is saying.

"I'm one of them," she adds.

I don't say anything. There is no need. Everyone knows Hutton and the kids he has brought through. She is waiting though, for whatever questions she thinks I have, or the facts I might tell her. But I have nothing I want to know.

"No questions or anything?" she asks.

I shrug.

"You seem cool to me," I say. "And I already told you I like Hutton. Nothing else sounds relevant. He's Fostered a lot of kids. I don't really know many."

I'm not sure if she likes what I said, or why she wouldn't. I was being genuine. It doesn't matter at all. I don't want to be judged on anything other than me. I can't go doing the opposite for others.

"I come up here a lot," she says. "I like the spot. I'd buy that house if I could. Live up here and avoid everyone until I needed the company."

"Sounds perfect."

She smiles at this.

"I'd let you visit," she says.

"I wouldn't leave."

She laughs again and I notice how she has different levels. This one is genuine, a real happy. Others are forced like she feels the need to make a noise at something she doesn't really like. As if she wants others to feel better no matter what.

"I don't like you that much," she tells me.

She stands and tells me to follow and she walks toward the edge of the cliff.

We stand looking down to the cove below, a small beach, blocked on all sides, accessible by boat or the smugglers tunnel that runs through the cliff. I don't know why I ask. But Sarah smiles, big and happy like she is proud of the connection.

"Do you know Serge?" I ask.

"Everyone knows Serge," she says.

And they do.

"He still lives there," she tells me. "Over eighteen. Not part of the system. But he stayed."

I stare at her again.

"Serge said it was time to go. Said he'd pop up, weekends mostly. Hutton said he didn't have to go."

"You two get on?"

"Why is that a surprise?"

I think about this and the only reason is because of the age. Because Serge is cool and Hutton is not.

"I don't know," I lie.

We walk the edge making sure there is a gap so if we stumble we don't fall.

13.45 p.m.

I think to the day when Darren came home, his shirt ripped, an eye swelling and scratches on his face and neck and blood on his white shirt. Quinn had laughed as Darren in his school uniform walked in. Laughed at the fact his son had ended up looking that way.

"Looks like someone handed you your arse," Quinn said, laughing and being joined by the cackle of my mum.

Darren had his head down and walked for the hall and the stairs. But Quinn grabbed him by the shirt on his shoulder and pushed him up against the wall to the outside. Darren was smaller then, at least that's how I see it. Pushed up against a wall by a man his physical superior, a man who he feared and hated in measures he didn't need to number.

"Did you cry?" Quinn asked, his face pushed up against his son's. "I bet you did. Got beat and then you cried."

I watched as Darren stared at Quinn, looked right into his eyes and grinned. He knew he was a disappointment and he knew this made him feel good.

"Don't smile at me," Quinn said.

But Darren kept his smile, as Quinn pushed harder into his body, his fist balling up, and Darren not pushing back. All he had as an attack was the face of happiness.

Quinn pushed and forced Darren to the side and down, and Darren stumbled away.

"Embarrassed," Quinn said. "I'm embarrassed to be your dad. You get that?"

Darren just smiled, and stepped toward the stairs.

"Don't walk away, grinning like some idiot. You need to apologise. To me. I can't have this. Not on my name."

Darren stopped and looked at him.

"I'm ever so sorry," he said, his teeth visible between his lips.

He knew what was coming, maybe not exactly how, but the force he knew about all the time.

"The hell you are, you little-."

Quinn didn't finish, Darren swung short and sharp and caught Quinn on the cheek. Quinn's head flashed left and as he looked back, he threw a short right hook that hit flush and Darren dropped. Not out cold but as near to it as make no difference. He tried to lift himself but had no idea of which direction that would be. He fell face down, tried to get up again and slouched back. He rolled over onto his back and Quinn laughed.

There were three ways for Darren to make sense of that. Three people to blame for the assault. Himself, Quinn or the kid that beat him. He chose the last and came after Serge, and just kept on losing, and Quinn kept on punishing.

Darren wanted revenge on a boy who was his physical superior and respect from a man who should love unconditionally but had no feelings at all. You can't claw your way out of that, no matter how many times you try to beat the odds. There is no chance those two events happen in succession, no chance either happens at all.

13.50 p.m.

The smuggler's tunnel is two people wide most of the way. It slopes down and bends left and right and needs lighting all day because the place is dark. There are puddles and damp, not from tide rising but water seeping through from above. It isn't what it once was, a natural fissure in the rock where sailors on wooden ships hauled stolen goods and brought in illegal merchandise to sell without tax. That was a long time ago when the town was a village and the land around unfarmed and unused. It is a reinforced tunnel to a beach of natural beauty. Locals claim it as their own, a place where tourists are not welcome. The beach is brown sand that turns your feet dirty, like all the sand on this coast. At least I assume it is, I have never been through here before.

"Not once?" Sarah asks.

I shake my head.

I don't like the enclosed space, the smell of the sea, and sand under my feet. It is a concrete floor but through wind, and waves and people, the floor is rough and cracked and broken.

I feel enclosed, not something I like. Sarah walks and after what seems like minutes we hit some stone steps, still enclosed, still with the arch a foot above my head. Water drips and runs down the walls.

"It's safe," she says. "It has never collapsed. Not even back in the day."

At the bottom of the stairs the tunnel bends right and we walk and I see the exit, a bar stopping people from running straight out. I've only seen photos of here. I think I am one of the few locals who have never set foot on this sand. We step out into fresh air but are still five metres above the beach. There are steps down, steps that are crumbling on the edges, with algae covering the edge and a line from the water running out of the tunnel and over concrete.

The sand is brown but it has more pebbles than on the main sea-front, like a poor quality of gravel. Sarah holds her hands out to her side and inhales deeply. The place is deserted, not another person to see or hear. The beach larger than it looked from above, a space to hold a festival, the water out, the sun warming but not heating. The smell a perfect presentation of the town. The wind is hidden, no breeze at all, a protection from the rocks and cliff face that juts out on both sides into the sea.

"Your brother still want to kill him?" Sarah asks.

"Maybe," I say. "Can't see it happening. Quinn wouldn't live it down."

"He sounds quite the man."

"No man at all."

"He's known for fighting."

I laugh at this, because this is what Quinn wants people to think, people to believe.

"He is known for losing. He'll fight you. But he hasn't beat anyone of note. Wouldn't fight anyone he thought could beat him, not fair. Not straight up. Man is a coward. And sometime soon Darren will take him."

"And the world will be right?"

"The world will just have Darren taking Quinn's place. Another nobody believing they are something and everyone looking on laughing at the idiot."

"And you?"

"I'll keep quiet until I can leave. Easy really. Time is what it takes."

"It takes more than that," she says. "A whole lot more to escape."

There is no reason for me to say, and you would know that how? Because her face and voice tell me experience backs her words, a life I don't want to know. There is no reason you can define as good for her to be cared for by Hutton. No one he cares for is there because they had a lovely life.

"Are you out?" I ask.

"Enough to make it seem it is the past. But it isn't. It is always going to be a part of the present no matter how long I live. And besides I didn't break free, I was pushed away."

14.10 p.m.

"Why have you never been here? It was one of the first places Hutton brought me, Serge brought me down too, showed me round. Said this was the best part of the town. I'd never really been to the sea."

I had never thought, never really cared. It is part of my life as it is. Places like this aren't for me, aren't the experiences people want me to live.

"No one wanted to bring me," I say. "And it is a place with a lot of people. I don't know. It just never happened."

She turns to me and smiles.

"Well, I'm showing you. So when someone asks have you been to the cove, you can say, yeah, Sarah brought me."

"And they'll all know who Sarah is?" I ask.

She laughs.

"No, but they will want to find out, and maybe that is better."

We stand in silence and watch the water and the small waves that seem to come in through sets of four. Four crashes and then a silence and a pause and then four more. I could be wrong, seeing a pattern where none exists. We stand and watch and listen and feel the wind and a little spray from the sea hit our faces. I could be alone but I'm glad I'm not. I don't look at her and I don't think she looks at me. We stand and inhale deeply over and over for minutes that seem like hours and are filled with everything I want.

"You want to see where I live?" Sarah asks.

14.40 p.m.

The phone is ringing as Sarah opens the door to Hutton's house with the key she has.

"That will be for me," she says.

The house is huge, a real old building that should, and maybe was, a bed and breakfast. It has wood in triangles near the roof and huge windows, the old kind, sash I think they are called. They slide up and don't open out. The hallway is as big as the first floor to my council house and the whole thing just gets bigger. Rooms as big as the ground floor on anything built on my estate.

The furniture old, but not antique, just used and comfortable and not something you can buy new. There are stairs that double back half-way up and are as wide as a car. From outside I saw three floors.

The phone is on a table at the foot of the stairs. In my house it is on a small table next to a small seat in the front room. If anyone could call that is where I'd answer and speak. No one ever calls for me, and quite frankly no one ever calls for anyone. I haven't heard the thing ring in more than a year.

Sarah picks up the phone and places it to her ear.

"Yeah, it's me. Sorry. I know. I just wanted to get out."

There is a pause when the other person speaks and she turns to me.

"No," she says. "I don't know where Billy went."

The stairs, I see, don't have carpet that covers all the exposed wood, just a strip down the middle, a strip as wide as I am tall, held down with a brass bar on every step. The walls are covered in patterned paper that has a 3-D edge of something that looks like a combination between a spade and a club on a playing card.

"I'm going to stay here," she says. "Sorry. Honestly. I just had a moment. Kind of just thought I needed to get out."

The other person speaks again.

"I don't know where he went," she says. "Home maybe? He didn't say."

The other voice speaks again.

"I'll stay here," she says. "I promise."

I am in Hutton's house, which is strange in itself. I knew where he lived, I knew the house. It is too far from where I live to be a place I'd accidentally walk by. I don't know who lives here, although we all know it a foster house for teens. Hutton sure puts in the hours. Sarah and Hutton, and I assume his wife. He is a good guy but not enough for me to care about who and what he is outside of school.

"How many of you are there?" I ask, looking round, staring at the high ceilings, in awe of how much space there is. There are four in my house and we all fit into a tiny box.

"Four kids," she says. "Well, four kids and Hutton and Serge. And another."

She walks down the corridor and I follow past a room with a TV and sofas. Everything seems big, the furniture, the spaces, the ornaments. It feels like the house for a giant. The doorways wider and taller, the ceilings too high, impossible to jump and touch.

"Beautiful place, isn't it?" she says.

I just nod my head and look at it all. It could be an historical homage to an old scientist, Newton's house, or maybe even

Einstein's home. It isn't museum standard as it is lived in, but it is, to me, a place that makes me smile.

"Was it Hutton?" I ask. "On the phone?"

She nods and smiles that perfected smile of guilty but let me free because I am sweet and innocent.

"I always come back here when I run. I don't do it often, not now, but I used to."

"Why didn't you tell him I was here?"

"Because that would break the rules. And he'd come. And that would mean trouble. He likes you."

"What does that mean?"

"Exactly what I said. He likes you. He is pretty good at figuring people out, knowing who they really are. And believe me I've tried to make him hate me. But I'm glad he doesn't."

"I don't think I'll be moving in anytime soon."

She laughs at this.

"It's actually OK. No need to run. Can't imagine there will be any place better."

"Why are you here?"

She looks at me, lowers her eyelids, tilts her head to the side and waits, thinking.

"Not important," she says.

14.50 p.m.

Sarah pushes on a door at the back of the house. We step into a huge room, a bar at one end and a pool table taking up the middle. Not a cheap table, one of the real heavy pub tables. The green cloth looks worn, the carpet around its feet and edges, flat and discoloured. It is what I imagine it to be: a teen playroom. Anything else and there would be a fruit machine and arcade game. I look and there is a dartboard with a long rubber matt with white lines telling you where to stand.

It all looks well used.

"Can you play?" Sarah asks.

The truth is, I don't know. I have seen it played, a few times. I've seen snooker on TV. I have seen people do it. But just like the darts, I have an idea of what needs to be done, I just don't know if I can put those simple moves together and do it.

"I've never tried," I tell her.

"I thought all boys believed themselves to be the best player they know."

"Not me. I'd say I'm the only boy who doesn't know how to play."

"Football?"

"Nope."

"Rugby?"

"Not a clue."

"You sure you are from around here?" she asks giggling. "Those, with the addition of cards and beer, are the way of life."

"Fishing?" I ask, because many do this too.

"There is that. Do you fish?"

"Not once."

She hands me a cue and starts sticking yellow and red balls into a triangle.

"You know the rules, right?"

I shake my head.

"Not a clue," I say.

"You have led a sheltered life."

The rules, she explains, occasionally. I don't get it, and it turns out I don't know how to hold a cue. I can hit the white, and it moves, but not necessarily in the direction I want. Hitting a red ball, because that is what I have, for a reason I have yet to grasp, the colour I need to pot. Angles are tricky, where to hit and where to connect not something that is immediately obvious. I don't know where to focus. Do I look at the ball, the cue or where it is going? I don't know, so I change each time with the same pathetic outcome.

Sarah is good, and in comparison, to me, a phenomenon. She pots balls, sets things up and leaves me with tricky shots. I am an embarrassment to the game and myself.

She pots the black and I have five balls remaining. One of them Sarah potted off the break, and another went in when I hit a ball and missed but it somehow hit two cushions and went in the middle. That is my highest break in my life. One ball, by chance. And I think, in old age this will still be the case.

Sarah stands looking at me, leaning on her cue.

"You are actually the worst player I have ever seen."

"Thank you," I say and she smiles, that happy genuine smile. "This will live long in the memory as I am never going to play again."

15.20 p.m.

Sarah's face falls and she swears. I hear it too, the front door she had closed, is opened and hitting the chain. There are other ways in, there must be. Having a house like this, with the kids who stay, shouldn't have the possibility of locking people out from the inside. The door is pushed three times, the person checking if the chain is really there.

"Sarah," the voice comes. "Open the door."

It isn't angry, but it is loud. A huge booming deep tone. I watch Sarah's face and she relaxes to a degree, smiles a little too as she releases her held breath.

"Serge," she says, to no one but herself.

I wait in the pool room, watching the door and Sarah is back quickly, Serge at her side. He isn't a huge kid, wiry would be closer to correct than massive. But his dirty T-shirt reveals arms that have work in them, and shoulders and back that are broad through genes and exercise. He stands about six-feet tall and would be a quarterback in any American movie.

"Jim said you were on your own," he says, speaking to Sarah but looking at me.

"I lied," Sarah says, wincing as if her honesty hurts.

"And who are you?" he asks me.

"I'm Billy," I tell him, not moving or holding out a hand.

He stares at me, up and down with his eyes like most people do.

"Greegan," Sarah says.

This word, my surname changes everything. Serge's face stiffens and his eyes go a way to closing. I see the tensing in his body, the same stiffness I see in Quinn before he throws hands at people.

"You anything like your brother?" Serge asks.

"I don't want to be."

"Going to cause me trouble?"

"Wouldn't want to."

"Me and your brother have history. One where he loses."

"He is Ok, Serge," Sarah says.

"Been said before, and often not true. They said it about me and look where that ended."

Serge turns to Sarah.

"Why?" he asks.

"Don't know, we just made the decision and ran."

Serge rubs his face.

"You don't need to do that anymore, you don't need to push and fight and do everything you can to make people push you away."

"I'm not trying to cause trouble," she says.

"So you bring Darren's brother here?"

"I didn't know you would be coming back."

"And that makes you feel better?"

It sounds like a father scolding a daughter.

"That's not what it is," she says.

They stare at each other, Sarah, swallowing saliva, Serge just watching and thinking.

"I took him down to the cove," she says. "Like you did with me."

Serge ignores her and his attention and eyes are on me.

"I don't like your brother," Serge says. "At all. But I guess you know that."

I nod because I do. No one speaks and we stand and wait and watch Serge looking at us.

"But I don't think you hate him as much as me," I say.

"And I guess you don't hate him as much as you do Quinn," he tells me.

I shake my head, which is strange because this means it is true.

Serge looks down at the floor, the threadbare carpet and wipes his palms down the side of his shirt and trousers.

"Jim told me to come up and make sure you were home," he says. "Make sure everything was safe. You can't keep doing this. This is not how it works."

"Got you an afternoon off work," Sarah says, the cheek back into her voice.

"To babysit," Serge tells her.

15.50 p.m.

They play and I watch, and no one asks me to leave. The bar has water and squash, and glasses I have never seen before. They are thick, chunky and heavy. The glass slightly green or blue depending on how the light hits them. Serge wins, occasionally Sarah takes a frame, but it is because Serge pots the black when he shouldn't, or Sarah goes on a run. Over ten games Sarah has no chance.

The clock on the wall ticks past the time School ends. There are snacks of crisps and nuts. It is a mini-bar for kids. In the past it might have been for adults, with optics. The beer towels remain, and there are beer mats too. It is like those kitchens, and cookers parents buy for children, a practice run at adult life in bright plastic.

Here there is everything you need to understand pub life with the exception of alcohol.

They talk about everything and nothing, insulting each other and laughing at themselves. I watch, not able to join in because I don't have their history and I don't know, not really, who they are. The smashing noise of a big break, or a shot hoping on luck. "Just smack it," a tactic Sarah uses, and sometimes it pays off.

I refuse the offer to play, because I can't. I don't know how and joining in would slow things down. So I watch, on a stool, at a fake bar like an old man watching the youngsters, waiting for a moment to start a small hustle. But I don't have one, I just have the ability to watch in silence and smile at this life they have.

They know I am there, but it is like they are performing, and I have paid to watch, and all I see is what they want to show, and it seems like a theme of happiness. But soon, I know, I have to go and all of this, all this strange set-up, this different world with people I barely know speaking and joking like they have been doing the same all their life will no longer be there. I will have my own home, my own reality, and my own need to hide out in the open.

I look at the time and wonder about the evening. Darren will be there, someone might come and speak, someone in uniform, someone to caution or talk. But that is it. There will be an official threat, a consequence if he repeats or does something that they deem illegal but not quite. But he won't listen, he'll talk back and the uniforms, if they don't know him well, won't handle it and have no idea what to do with the kid who has no respect. Quinn might shout, but probably won't even come to the door. They will have their bond, their united front against the uniforms who try to impose order. They will laugh at how they can treat them with contempt, and they will look at me and laugh.

I hear the door before them. They are lost in the game, and Sarah takes any small victory as bigger than it is. Anything to have one small dent in the armour Serge has around him. He is untouchable, for now, at this age. I don't know what he does, but it is manual. His clothes say as much. The cargo trousers covered in dust, the black shirt that is thick material designed not to fray or rip. His hands are dirty, the finger nails I saw when he held a glass as dirty as mine when I used to dig up worms.

I see the movement in the corner of my eye, at least I think I do. Some of the spiritual people might say I felt it. Whatever the cause I turn to look, not in anger or curiosity, just because something in my brain says I should. It doesn't register at first, not what I see or what it means. I stare and I am smiling, and then I understand and I widen my eyes, stand up from the stool and step back. Sarah sees me first, she pulls up from the shot she is taking, looking at me and in turn Serge sees her and looks my way. I step back, further from the window. I lift my hand, point my finger.

"Darren," I say.

He is staring back, his face up close to the glass. His eyes are wide and he scrunches his face. He is the same as this morning. The same clothes, the same bag, the same look, like someone scared but unable to run.

"Billy," he shouts and the sound makes its way through the glass.

I stand still, looking through the window, into the back garden, the large green rectangle of striped lawn.

"You do this?" Serge asks me.

I shake my head, I have nothing to say.

"The same as at school," Sarah says.

"What?" Serge asks, sharp and curt. "What the hell are you talking about?"

No one answers as we hear the front door pushed, opened and then caught on a chain. Sarah lets out a scream.

"Stay here," Serge tells us.

But we don't, we follow him out of the room. He is fast and turns left away from the noise.

"Don't go outside," Serge tells us.

We walk down the corridor and see the front door pushed and pulled, one way to the limit of the chain and the other to the frame. I see Darren's face peering in on every push.

"What are you doing there Billy?" he shouts. "Let me in."

Sarah grabs my shirt, pulls me back.

"I'm not letting him in," I tell her.

She doesn't answer but she doesn't let go.

Darren pushes the door again, his face peering through the crack, he opens his mouth, his face red but he shoots back out of sight.

Sarah swears, lets me go and we rush to door.

We can hear Darren swearing and Serge talking calmly. Sarah lifts the chain off its hook, the front door free to open wide.

"What are you doing?" I say.

She doesn't answer not with words, she smiles at me in a way she hasn't shown before. But I have known her a day, or half a one. This could be how she shows her fear. I step forward as she opens the front door and we look out as Serge stands, side-on to Darren. This is an old scene played out as new. A couple of years ago at school this would have been how Serge showed everyone he was top man. Here with them each at eighteen, the school fights are something else, something more serious.

"Take it down there, Darren," Serge says. "I don't know what's going on, but think. Think about what's happening, who we are. This isn't school anymore."

Darren has seen Sarah open the door. There was a flash of anger, the consequence of disrespect from someone he sees as younger, someone who should do what he says. Serge is edging sideways, not crossing his legs or feet, a slow shuffle to the side like a slow motion ballerina. He is moving to put himself between Darren and the door. He always has his left shoulder forward, his right leg back. A stance he knows and in which he feels comfortable.

I watch Darren more than Serge. He seems twitchy, the agitated ticks of someone under stress. He twitches his head, looking around but in short snaps rather than panoramic flow. His hands move forward and back, open not clenched. He looks like someone trying to dance to a song they have never heard before, waiting for recognisable notes to move his body. Only the notes don't come in harmony.

"You'll come down, Darren," Serge says. "Time, and you'll come back down."

I look again and see the twitches for what they are. Darren is chewing, but there is nothing there to chew. His eyes popping open, the black pupils taking up all the colour.

"Billy," Darren shouts.

"He isn't coming out," Serge says.

"Billy, "he calls again.

Sarah looks at me, and tilts her head to the left. There is a question there but I don't know which one. Are you dumb enough to do this? Or are you too cowardly to do anything?

I don't know the answer and I don't know the question. I don't know Sarah. I don't know too much at all. Some history, mostly local, how to speak, although not enough words or confidence to make a point when challenged. I can walk, and breathe, and all the other basics. But what do I know? Really know? Nothing beyond I don't like it all, not any of it. I know I have very little future, that is apparent. I have no way of making grades in exams that require knowledge I don't have. It is my fault, I can accept that. I have done nothing, not listened, not been there, not wanted to build. But I have other things, a mind full of thoughts about the day, about whose home I live in, about what they are and what they do and what that will mean to me. I know all these things. They are specific though, specific to me, and now, and them and what state they are in.

    I think of the time we went out for the day. Quinn had money and what better way to spend it than on a trip to the holidaymaker's places of beer gardens, picnic tables and roasting flesh. Quinn had drunk, the money won, or stolen, or something. It certainly wasn't earned. But there was plenty of it. He drank and spoke and joked and was loud and fun. That loudness of a man just the right side of insulting. Playful even. He knew what he wanted from the day and violence wasn't one. He wanted to drink and look and feel like normal people. The normal he liked, the normal that means a sleeveless top, and shorts and socks and trainers in a pub garden drinking pints and enjoying life. He wanted some of that, wanted to see if he could be that way, could be part of it all. He had the money to do it so he tried to fit in. It was a town along the coast, two towns down, or maybe three. Fewer people to know him and us, fewer people to judge him on what he was and is. We had drunk too, me and Darren. Fizzy drinks, and eaten crisps and played around, other kids too, on swings and slides and climbing frames. We were another family, parents getting toasted on sun and alcohol, and kids running free. It is what everyone was doing.

We walked back to the bus stop, no driving for Quinn. I don't know why, he has never had a car, never known him to talk about if he could. Possible he never learned, possible he is permanently banned. What is sure, the reason will be no good.

We saw the bus moving away, and Quinn walked into the road, waving and laughing and joking, trying to get the small bus to stop. And it did, and he stepped on and said his thanks and laughed and joked and we all found seats and rested our legs, and they their livers. And we set off, driving back.

But Quinn's bladder couldn't hold out. He shouted for the bus to stop as we were weaving through lanes, the driver kept on going, laughing still because Quinn had shown him nothing but funny. The people on there with us, three young lads, an old couple and a single man no one wanted to sit near all looked and all knew and all saw.

Quinn started to shift and wriggle and I knew, and so did Darren and so did my mum. But she just smiled because this was Quinn, her man, the guy who stayed, and that is all that matters.

Quinn shouted again to stop the bus and the driver answered that they couldn't. Quinn swore, a long line of insults, fidgeting about, struggling, not able to hold things in, not able to control the basic emotion of need. He stood, legs close together, his face a comic picture of pain. He struggled up the aisle, stood and leaned into the driver, reached across and grabbed at the wheel. He swore and told the driver to pull over, and he did.

Quinn swore again and told the driver to wait. The door popped open, Quinn jumped out, took a step, undoing his zip, weeing on himself as he walked and released the pressure. The driver closed the door, accelerated and drove off. The three young lads cheered and laughed.

"Do you want to get out as well?" the driver shouted.

My mum stood and indicated me and Darren should follow. She walked up to the front of the bus and said nothing but nodded her head. The driver slowed, let us out, closed the door and drove off. Quinn was chasing down the road about as fast and as comfortable as a man in a three-legged race. The front of his shorts looking damp, his face red, and his fists clenched.

That is my memory. That is my day out. That is the fun we had, the day-trip of everything. A pleasure followed by chaos and carnage and insults and threats. A day where we were normal, a day where we couldn't keep up the act, a day where we stopped even trying. What was the point? We couldn't be them, shouldn't even try. We were us, the Greegans and that meant we were to stay away and not be part of anything but hate.

16.00 p.m.

"You ok?" Sarah asks.

I snap out of my mind and see Darren, his face red, swing at Serge. Serge blocks the shot, grabs Darren's arm, spins a little, drives his hip into Darren's, bends forward and flips Darren over, onto his back, the air pushed out, and no need for a follow up attack.

"You can't beat me, Darren," Serge says. "You tried for a long time and it always ends this way. There is nothing here. No point to this."

Darren stays on his back looking up and laughing. Serge has stepped back, looking down at this idiot, the guy who will take his beating but just keep trying, looking for that one grasp at luck, the one chance of winning that might fall his way by chance.

"Get going Darren," Serge says. "You are going to bring nothing but problems if you stay. We aren't at school anymore. None of this is important, none of this is normal."

"Normal," Darren says, and laughs again. "Not normal."

"What is wrong with you?" Serge asks, not looking for a reply. "Look where you are, on your back in a garden, put there by me. For what? Nothing. Move on. Do something other than try and balance out insults from your past."

Darren laughs again, laying like a starfish on the grass, a small holdall grasped in his left hand.

"Do you want me to apologise for what happened, what, three years ago?" Serge asks. "I'm sorry. I went too far, I shouldn't have done it. Genuinely. I'm sorry. I don't want to keep doing this."

Darren's humour changes, gone in an instant on the words

"I don't need an apology," he says. "I don't need another sorry."

Darren starts to stand, pushing his hands on the floor, his left not letting go of the bag. He stumbles forward, taking quick steps to stay upright, but he fails and slides forward, face down, his hands out in front. He swears at himself, or the ground, or the universe. He stands again, slowly, making sure he doesn't fall. He is near the gate that leads out onto the road. Facing the wrong way, he turns.

"What are you doing here Billy?" he shouts. "These aren't our people."

I don't say anything. He isn't my people, no one is. I don't have people. Relatives who I never see, never hear and no one speaks about any of them. I have no people at all. I'm stood next to a girl I met this morning, a girl I didn't even know was still in my school. A girl I thought had moved on months ago. Another of the failures of this house. I've spoken more to her today than anyone else, all of them combined, in the last month, and I still don't know her. She doesn't know me.

I feel her looking at me, the red-head, the really red hair glistening. Serge is looking only at Darren, standing side on, waiting to react to anything the man he has beaten so many times might try.

"There is no one for us, Billy," Darren shouts. "No one at all. Just me and you. Your mum, Quinn, they aren't there for us. You understand what I'm saying? There is no one for us."

We stand and listen and watch him shout and twitch and edge away. The bag in his hand he holds tight.

"Why are you here Darren?" I ask.

"To do something stupid. Something I thought I needed to do," he says, closing his eyes, his head falling forward.

"You've done enough, Darren," Serge says.

Darren lifts his head and stares at Serge. He smiles, in a way I haven't seen before. Something real.

"I've done a lot more than enough," he says.

16.10 p.m.

We stand around the pool table and Sarah is picking up the yellows and pushing them across the green cover, smacking them into other balls and some of them drop into pockets and I can hear them run through the mechanism inside until they fall to rest in the long waiting queue for the next person to push on the slider mechanism.

"You going to tell Jim?" Sarah asks.

Serge looks down and shakes his head.

"He'd shut it all down," Serge says. "The evening won't happen. I don't think you'll be allowed out anyways."

"I'll get out," Sarah says.

"Stop causing yourself trouble," Serge tells her. "This place is as good as you or I can get. Better than anything else I had. Don't blow it. I get it, I understand. But all this, it is a way out."

"Like you are out?" she says.

"Like I am out, yes."

"You aren't," she tells him. "You are just part of it."

"That's the point. I am part of it. Part of something. I've never been before. And now I am. And you think you can just keep being you. Doing what you want, being the loner with an attitude. No one can hurt you if you don't let them close, right? I get it. But you are wrong."

I am stood, trying to be nothing in a corner, trying as I always do, to be absent while I am there. I am watching and listening. Serge is not who I thought. I had him figured for a man of fighting, and he can, I know that. But he talks too, has other ways rather than throwing hands at any problem he sees in his way.

"No one wanted you. We know that. You accept that. No one wanted me either. That's why you and me are here," Serge says.

"It isn't the same," Sarah says.

"Nothing, no two people experience the same. But we are pretty close to be grouped together. That is why we both ended up here."

"The place of the great saviour. Big Jim."

Serge laughs.

"He is no saviour," he says, "no messenger from god. But he is a good man. He gives chances. You just have to be smart enough to take them. It is ok to be scared. Be afraid of adults offering something for nothing."

"He wants nothing in return?" she asks.

"I don't know what your experiences are, but he does want something. He wants to feel better about himself. So he doesn't do all this for no benefit. He does it to feel better, about what, I don't know."

"Not everyone comes out of here like you," Sarah says.

"Nobody wants them to. But you have the best chance to get out of here better. Stop trying to make that impossible."

"I'm still coming tonight," she says. "No matter what."

She turns to me.

"You want to come too, Billy?"

Serge swears.

"You can't do it, can you?" he says.

"Come where?" I ask.

"There is a small gathering tonight," Serge says. "Down in the cove. Nothing big. A few of us-"

"Including me," Sarah adds.

"-a few of us, a fire and some music. Happens now and again. I'm sure Sarah would tell you all anyway. We get left alone mostly. If either of you mess this up,"

"You'll be very angry."

"You'll achieve everything you want and be hated by those who cut you a break."

Serge stares at Sarah saying this. She tries to fight back with a stare of her own, a smirk on her face but she sees it and feels it as much as me. She moves her eyes down, and her smile hides away.

"Which means you need to move, Billy," Serge tells me. "You were never here, not that we know, and not that you'd admit. If you tell anyone about the cove, you have me to deal with. Cause any trouble, and the same. That is a threat. But it is also a fact. That will happen. You get me?"

I nod.

"It's ok," I say, because I know I will not go, that I can't go, that Quinn won't allow it, and if I snuck out, I'd earn a hiding, and days of pain, and punishment. I don't have those options, I don't have those freedoms.

16.20 p.m.

I walk around the lanes of the town, the short cuts through alleyways, the paths worn through grass and verges. I am going nowhere but in circles. I have to go home at some point. Dinner will be laid, and if I miss it, I don't eat because someone else will have what is served. Those are the rules. We all eat quick because we know someone will steal if we are slow. Quinn reaching across saying, "well, if you don't want it," and taking meat or chips or anything from your plate. I have to get back for that. If I want to eat. No raiding cupboards to make up, no staring into a refrigerator to choose what I can have to fill me up. There are times and there are rules and there are punishments.

But I don't want to go back. The day, and Darren, and the way he looked, the way he rocked. The fact he has missed work, the idea he has roamed around town looking to come down from his high, something he would have taken in the morning after Quinn beat him down. Maybe he stole some from Quinn, which means an evening of shouts and violence. Maybe Quinn knows he skipped work and lost money. There are a million possibilities and none of them good. I walk and avoid people, hitting the fields that run through the middle of two estates. Areas left without houses, but not without people. Teens go to drink and adults walk their dogs, and trees grow without being cut back and people still leave rubbish.

I walk through them all, and while I don't remember thinking this is where I wanted to be, it is where I am all the same. This little place, under trees with branches and leaves that grow straight up high and bend down and hit the ground. You can sit under them in the cold shade, and you can't be seen from paths or fields. Kids come under and drink and smoke, and cans and cigarettes are on the ground. They used to try and set fires, not for warmth, just to be cool. But no one ever really could, nothing proper, and I would see burned patches of mud, and the charred remains of paper and wood.

I came up here a lot. I think of it as my space, as my hide away. But it isn't, it is everyone's. Most teens this side of town have sat here, most teens had their first drink, first smoke and probably first kiss under here, or nearby. You can't get in by car, so there is a freedom. A brooke runs through it, hidden by brambles. There is a small wooden bridge to cross, although further down there are small stepping stones to skip across inch high streams. The water not deep, but clear and cold. A picturesque place in the middle of nowhere.

There is a football pitch up top, a level of rolled out field with goals either end, the field not official length and the white metal frames not the right size and the crossbars bent because kids hang from them.

I hear the voices, all young, split into two. The friends of encouragement and the enemies of insults. Two groups throwing words at each other but nothing physical. Groups who don't like each other, but groups who will switch allegiance in a moment if they are given the chance to win. I hear what they are saying, a game arranged, and battle drawn but through sport rather than a gang fight. Someone has decided to bring a ball.

The estates are either side, the boys split into two. It isn't fair, the advantage lies on the other side. The estate is bigger, there are more people, more families and more kids. A larger pool of talent, more people to make up the numbers. It happens regularly, and I have watched, although I can't see them from the window of my house. My bedroom is at the back and faces away. From the front I would be able to make out the game, the small figures running around, maybe even pick out a face or two.

Someone has rushed ahead, picked up a ball, and made it back. Two teams, not the best players they could pick, because those with a brain and a desire to play in real teams will avoid this game. Someone will get hurt, and someone will start swinging, and the result will mean nothing, and they will come back for more. I've watched, and girls will watch, and boys who hate the sport but love their estate will watch with the idea that honour is at stake. For them it is, for most it is a way to fight without fighting, a way to smash someone without having to hide from the police. It is a way to show those that watch who you are and where you fit in. It's like a coming out ball on a sporadic loop, everyone here deliberately on display, and selling themselves to whoever is interested for a moment or a lifetime together. Life-long loves are forming, and lifelong rivalries already playing out. The belief is they will be temporary, the reality is they fester forever.

    The estates can hear and some can see groups of kids mixing then splitting, and while they can't make out conversations, words and insults, they know what is happening, they know the day is about to have an extra hour delay to the norm. Some of the parents here will have done the same not so long ago, and some will have gone further, and some will be married to the people they watched or let watch them in school uniform barley more than half their young lives ago. Parents evenings with teachers who taught you and remember who and what you were, and believe they know that this defines who and what you, the child, will become.

This group of kids not ready to be adult but know the time is coming, have given me time to wait. They have through dumb, traditional rivalry, extended the deadline to get home.

I walk from my cover, bag over my shoulder to where they have gathered. Teams are being picked, and while there are enough to have two full games going on, they will struggle for numbers. At age fifteen and sixteen, the desire to kick a ball about in front of a crowd of peers is a low-level feeling. The downsides are huge, the embarrassment real, the possibility of losing face a constant fear for those who have spent years cultivating an image of cool and calm.

The two teams will consist of those who can play and those who destroy.

I hear the shouts and swearing, the teams and players being discussed, their qualification for participation a debate. This is the warm up, the pre-game rile, the small advantage sought out.

"He doesn't live up on your estate," a large lad called Mark shouts.

Mark is a rugby player by history and size. He can kick a ball, but he is nobody you'd call good.

The origin is a necessity, mostly. You have to be part of a number of streets to qualify to play. I live in the centre of one and I know most of the kids as we all went to primary, junior and high school together. A few moved on, a few moved away to more expensive houses, and they are all happy in the knowledge they don't get a free pass to selection. In other circumstances, faced with an out of town rival, everyone here would be united in their desire to smash them. But here and now, the only anger that can be found is against someone who for reasons beyond any control, lives across the valley. It all makes sense to everyone. It is the way of it.

I walk over to the edge of the pitch. There are no markings, no lines painted in. There are no areas to see, no defined space beyond two sets of goals. This adds to the confrontation, the arguments and pushing about if the ball is in or out of play, if the last one to touch it before it went over an imaginary line was you or them. We all have an idea where it should be, where we should sit and stand to watch, and groups, taking the side their houses sit, are spaced and waiting.

There are two groups in the centre of the field. I count them and there are fifteen boys, all in my year, none of them particularly known for their skill or finesse. None of them are on the way to a professional career in anything other than mundane boredom. They are arguing and there is one boy, a kid named Dan, a massive lad who has a career as a labourer stamped all over his life, just edging away.

"He doesn't live there anymore," Mark shouts. "He can't play."

Whatever the qualification rules are, and he does seem to be breaking some, the real point here is that Dan is actually quite good and also significantly stronger than anyone else on the pitch, Mark included, even if he would never admit that.

"We are one short," Pete tells him. "We aren't playing seven against eight."

"Find someone else then. Dan isn't playing. There's plenty from up your way."

"Who? No one is playing."

"Don't care."

Pete swears and looks around the side of the field with his estate. I smile, all the heads shaking, all the kids refusing to play with a look.

Mark walks over.

"One of you, get up and play. We haven't got time for this."

A few kids, the ones who fancy their chances against Mark, and those who just think he is a nobody with an anger problem, tell him to do one with swear words and insults. Mark bites but stays quiet. He knows he can't take them all and he knows they aren't scared, not in numbers and not alone.

"You," he says, pointing at me. "Greegan. You play."

"Get lost, Mark. He can't play," Pete says. "He'd get pushed around by the first years."

"You need someone, or you play with seven. And none of the cowards on your estate fancy it."

"Shut up, you dick," a girl says, and because she is female Mark has no answer.

Pete and Mark stare at each other.

"Bullshit cheating, Mark."

"Not my problem, mate. Greegan or seven. Your choice. Unless you can convince any of these flowers to play."

Pete swears looks at the crowd, knows no one is standing up. They are there to watch, too old to play and too cool to try. Pete looks my way, that face of predicted disappointment etched into a mask that tries for warmth.

"You in, Billy?" he asks. "Can you actually play?"

The answer is I can't. I've kicked a ball, had to suffer PE lessons back in the day. But I'm no player and they all know it, and they all smile, both sides, each of them seeing me as the masterstroke joke.

Pete puts his hand on my shoulder, and I think the only other time this kid has touched me was to push me out the way, or move me from near him because he just doesn't give a shit.

I look at him, not really needing to answer. We all know I can't.

"Stick you in goal?" Pete asks.

I want to say no, tell him to do one, to walk away. You never spoke to me other than to bully, other than to belittle and now you want me as a saviour to your own vanity project. He places his arm around my shoulder like a friend, only false. I drop my bag on the ground and walk with him.

"Just get in the way of anything. Don't be scared," Pete says. "It's a ball. It hurts, but not much and not for long. Ok? You know the rules right?"

I say nothing but just nod. I realise I have said nothing to him. I know he thinks me the dumbest thing on the field.

Everyone is looking at me and laughing and smiling and Mark thinks he has made a genius move.

The kids on my team drift into places on the field, places they instinctively know, and feel is the right place to stand. I've seen enough to know most will chase the ball, a couple will sit back not wanting to run, and Pete will try tricks and avoid being kicked.

The game starts and I know the names of players on each team. I can't be sure I will in a few years' time. There were kids in my primary school, kids I would have played with and spoken to, but they left and their faces are in the photos yet their names are no longer in my head. Either my young brain is shot or I care little about things.

There is shouting and swearing and an absence of encouragement. Motivation through insult, or rivalry though swearing. That is all there is. In their heads they are seeing their game as if played by smooth professional men they have watched in countless games on TV. But they are uncoordinated boys with no hope of making the local team. They are acting out and the filter of their imagination makes them believe they are Greek gods on a small-town public-field.

Pete gets the ball and Mark chases him down for the two steps he needs while Pete tries to get the ball under control. Mark uses his leading right shoulder to go straight through Pete's back, sending him to the ground. Mark gets the ball, turns and smacks it forward. There is no finesse, no actual aim, and no player near to where the ball finally bounces.

"That's a foul," Pete shouts from the ground.

"Get away with you, you big girl," Mark tells him before turning to the player on his team nearest the ball. "Chase it," he shouts again.

The ball is way too long and it comes near to me, I walk out of the goal under no pressure and I bend down reaching out with my hands.

"Don't pick it up," a tall boy named Richard shouts.

I look up, not understanding.

"You are out of your area," he tells me.

I look around and the goal is close to me, there are no markings I can see, but everyone agrees. I am not allowed to use my hands here.

I kick the ball as hard as I can and it manages to travel the few metres to Richard, rolling to his feet. It wasn't what I was planning, wasn't the direction I had wanted it to go. In my mind I had seen the ball flying up to the other end of the field, landing near Pete who would turn and score. But a long ball turned into a short, uncoordinated pass is good enough for us all.

Richard nods like I have done something to congratulate, turns and starts to run with the ball at his feet. Mark, like a terrier chasing balls in a park, hunts him down, sprinting in a mad release of adrenaline-hate directly to where he thinks Richard will be within three seconds. Richard has two options, pass and let someone else have Mark chase; slow up, brace and play the game of collision, or switch direction and let Mark sprint on by.

He chooses the first, but deliberately late, the ball pushing forward along the ground, down the side of the imagined pitch to a player on the wing. Mark doesn't deviate, knows he has sprinted for nothing, and clatters Richard a second after the ball has gone. Richard loses his feet and hits the ground, but bounces up quick. He stands tall and over Mark. Mark pushes him again but without venom, turning away and sprinting off, his energy depleting in visual steps, slowing and puffing.

I watch, the ball pinging around doing nothing, going nowhere but sideways, and staying within an area all the players can reach. A moveable human pinball machine, with feet as bumpers as no one can, and some don't dare, to control the ball and have it at their feet. It brings aggression and collision, and a knock and a fall. The ball bounces around, moving to people but not the ones intended. A boy tries a dribble and is upended, cries foul but the game moves on. The ball bounces around and then breaks free, into space, the other end of the field, away from me and away from my thoughts. A shout goes up, two boys jump, one reeling away and smiling.

"Goal," he shouts.

Mark looks on, trying to think of an excuse, a reason for contesting, but thinks of nothing as the smallest player on their team runs to collect the ball.

We restart and the game, after two passes back, collapses into the same set-up. A group coming ever closer from all sides, the ball pinging around, shouts and shoulder charges, kicks and pushes, as the ball is punted hard and in the direction of goals. Whatever defence my team has decided to take works as the ball never breaks free for long. Richard is quick, and catches any break before the other team can move. Collecting the ball, turning and hoofing it forward into the masses. He knows what he is doing, and they all want the same. A scrum of kids who can release physical force through a semi-regulated scuffle.

I think about the day, think about Serge and Sarah and their lives. I have no idea where they came from, and as little idea as they about where they will go. Serge seems to have tamed self-destruction, but he always had the quiet confidence of defence. I don't understand Sarah, the rebel at home with a teacher. A place, the house, the set-up. Settled and sure, and yet she runs and fights and pushes too. Not physical, not looking to hurt the body, just make sure everyone stays away. The way she looked at Serge, the way she listened. I have never seen it before, certainly never done it myself, never been where someone can be changed to the positive by being near another. I smile because her red hair is stupid, such a huge insult to everywhere she needs to be. I don't know what it was about, it certainly wasn't an interest in me for the romantic. There would be those who would confuse her attention as interest, or pretend not to see the obvious in how she was being nothing but someone to set fire to any calm. She wanted the adventure, not me. The way she looked at Serge was the way girls look at boys they love. In the eyes and the attention. She wanted to push back and she did but that is because it is all she knows. There are variations on what she does, changes to the level of contempt. I was just an interest, a day's project. I'm not stupid enough to think romance is budding. I'm stupid enough for a lot of other things, or lacking courage, or missing a foundation to strength. Something isn't there, something isn't right. I don't have something others possess.

 I hear the shout, my surname called by more than one. I smile as what can I do but acknowledge that is me. I look up and I see Mark sprinting toward me and the goal. The ball is moving toward me too, far in front of Mark, and far in front of me. If we were of equal speed, I would make it first. The distance to me is shorter and decreasing as the ball rolls forward. But we aren't the same speed and Mark is moving, sprinting with his face red and eyes wide and cheeks blowing; and I am standing still thinking of a girl I will never get to see again, not like today, not like anything. I hear my name again, shouted, the word run added to it now. I take a step, don't think and run, not looking at anything but the ball. I hit top speed which isn't fast, not in respect to those on the field and nothing compared to Mark.

    I don't see him now, just the ball and it coming closer. I run a few steps at speed and I dive forward and to my right, hands out, not caring for my clothes, not caring for anything other than grabbing the ball up into my chest as I slide forward on my side. I dart down, the ball hits my hands, I grab it up as I slide. But I see the feet, the shoes, soles up, two of them together, worn down, pressed together, both of them hitting my hands, pushing through, squeezing the ball up into my chest, the left one sliding off, moving up and pressing against my face. The contact making me spin, my legs travelling forward and around, my body going the other way like a propeller and my hips as the fulcrum. I spin, not knowing which direction, not knowing how far, fast, uncomfortable and in a haze. I stop and I wait for the pain but none comes. I lay still, holding the ball, cradled up into my chest. I bring my knees up and hold it with everything, like a baby curling up in a blanket. I feel the kick, open my eyes and look up. Mark is standing above me, his face red, his right foot going back and forward in short sharp pokes, kicking at the ball but only hitting my arms.

"He's out of his area," he shouts as he kicks again.

I try to stand but I won't let go of the ball. My balance not enough to get me to my feet. Mark kicks again but he misses as his body jerks to the side.

"Get off him," Richard says as he pushes Mark away.

Mark stumbles and turns and sees Richard looking down, chest puffed, his eyes staring into his face, daring him. Mark turns and reaches out to grab the ball, but I am holding onto it tight. He tries to shake my arms, and pull the ball, but I hold on. It isn't a test of strength, not a real one. It is his arms against my whole body. This is one I can win.

"He was out of his area," Mark says again.

"Bullshit," Richard tells him.

"It was a great save," Pete says. "And you are the one who fouled."

"It's a penalty," Mark says.

"That doesn't even make sense," Pete tells him. "If it was handball, which it wasn't, it was outside the area so it would be a free-kick."

"Give me the ball," Mark says.

I don't and he tries to pull it away again. I watch his face, looking into his eyes. With Quinn this would mean violence, a come back of a slap or punch. I know this, and Mark knows the reason I stare. He looks around, Richard too big, Pete too popular, and me, small and hated, and labelled and nothing. He swings, like a kid who can't fight and never really has. A long arching right hand that starts way back behind him and takes seconds to come round and hit the target. I see it, watch it all the way, ducking in time and watching the hand flash wildly over my head. The guy can't punch, but he is bigger and stronger so the next step is clear.

Mark loses his footing and stumbles around as his balance is shot from the momentum of his punch. Spectators laugh, and he hears like we all do, but only he burns with embarrassment. I pull my arm back and throw the ball as far as I can, which isn't miles, but it is enough not to be close, and not to be taken. Mark crouches and throws himself forward, hitting my stomach with his right shoulder and taking me off my feet. He lifts me up and drives me down. I know to relax, to just go loose, tightening up leads to injury. I hit the ground and Mark is on top of me. I am smiling because there is nothing else to do. I'm not trained or practiced in any moves to stop the attack. I don't have the strength to stop him, or the desire to try. He wraps his arms around my head and I feel his muscles tense as he squeezes. But his arms are in the wrong place, the pressure being applied to my nose and mouth rather than neck. It is uncomfortable and painful but I am not at risk of blacking out. He wriggles his arms and his skin rubs against that on my face. It will make me red. But I don't care. I could bite but that would only bring a temporary reprieve and then more anger, a surge in his adrenaline to bring stronger squeezes and harder blows.

Nobody tries to pull him free. There is no adult and we all know energy ebbs and tiredness comes and the spectacle is not something anyone needs to drag out. This is no Broadway show with a beginning, middle and end. This is a scuffle between a boy big enough to be a man and a little kid not strong enough to fight back. It started with the end and no one feels suspense at an unexpected twist or outcome. The longer he holds and the longer I don't respond the deeper the shame he will feel.

"Get off him, Mark," Pete says.

They are standing around, a circle, looking down, players on both teams, most smiling, all for different reasons. Some of it will be because they see humour in Greegan's little brother getting pain and payback for my brother's actions, as if I will pass this on in some physical way to a boy I hate more than them, to a boy they fear more than me.

Mark releases his hold and stands.

"It was a penalty," Mark says, but the conviction is gone, the moment passed and his friends are looking away and down. There is no support and he knows it.

One of the players jogs back with the ball. We are all stood around waiting for the decision, waiting for the debate on what happens next.

"It was a great save, you fouled. Our ball. Let's get going," Pete says.

The boys all nod, the heat all gone from the moment. They want to play and wait for the next blow up.

Mark swears at me and pushes me in the chest and I step back from the force. He points at me as he jogs backwards, but he turns and runs off taking up a position he has just created in the formation in his head.

"You Okay?" Pete asks me.

I nod.

"You don't say much," he says. "Good save that though. Any more and you'll be asked to join in all the time. Didn't know you were a crazy bastard. A bit like your brother after all."

"Nothing like him at all," I say.

Pete smiles.

"Good," he tells me.

16.30 p.m.

The game goes on, nothing good happening. Two shots come my way, I get my body in front of them and while I don't catch, the ball bounces free and Richard clears up. No one passes back, no one trusts my feet but I am in, Richard and Pete call me Billy, when the ball goes out of play I roll it to one of them. They shout my name, ask me for the ball, trust me to start the game, don't demand they take the goal kick, don't expect me to fail. Some kids wander off, bored with the show, not liking the lack of violence. There is still some, late tackles, shoulder charges and dirty kicks, but it is standard, a baseline of niggle that is expected. Nothing blows and Mark has calmed through fatigue. He sprints occasionally, bumps and punts the ball. But he is gone, the enthusiasm for destruction not even showing in his feigned aggression. The game fading out into a moment when someone will pretend they have forgotten the score and a 'next-goal-wins' shout will give an energy boost to the last minutes of play.

This is the first time I am part of it, involved to the end, part of the narrative when someone tells the story tomorrow.

And the story will be mine.

16.40 p.m.

I hear a scream, I look to the side of the field where those watching from my part of the estate are sat. The scream passes like a Mexican wave, kids standing and running, grabbing bags like they were all they had in the world, a possession for which to risk your life. The game carries on but in a small pocket. The kid with the ball and two or three around them oblivious to anything other than the game. The rest look and those few realise the competition has stopped. They look around, like we all do, trying to see the cause, trying to see what makes that many run. A wild dog, a rat, a kid with a firework. But it is none of those, I see in time with everyone else. But I feel it more, I see what is there, I know more than them, I have a greater connection. But I understand, just like them, nothing at all. I have a guess, a better ability to imagine. I have information they don't, experiences they will never gain. But it doesn't mean I am right, it doesn't mean I have figured it out, the reasons for why she is here and looking like human fear is not fact in my mind.

    Her face is set in one wide-eyed expression of seeing but not focusing. I've seen it before but not often and not prolonged. A brief moment of shock when realisation hits but it slips away when she thinks of a way to ignore the pain of what is there. She is lost, a mind reeling to make sense and finding none. She has blood covering her, splatters and smears. Red streaks she has wiped on her face and drips down her front. She is wearing a baggy t-shirt and grey trousers. In her left hand she is holding a knife, one I recognise from the kitchen, a plastic handle that has melted at the end, one kept sharp on one side, the point broken off. But she is holding it by the blade, clenching her hand and cutting her palm. Blood drops freely and she stumbles forward to where the crowd were. My mother staggering forward and a sea of teenagers running in fear.

The ball is picked up and everyone runs, not away, not fully, at least not all of them. The desire to be distant, to be far away but close enough to watch is strong, and groups huddle, gaining confidence in numbers and watch as they edge away, keeping a specified distance from my mother. They have guessed, and figured the space they need to keep, understood their speed in relation to the shuffling zombie with mad eyes. I feel a few looks my way, understand they know and connect me, because I am connected. She isn't a Greegan, no one knows her that way. But she is, more than me. She chose to take the name and the man. But the town already knew her and calling someone something new is a difficult step to take for most.

"Is everyone in your family a psycho?" Mark says, he is edging back, close to me but wanting more distance from my mother.

I look at him, think about who he is and what he will be. Maybe he'll change when thrown out into the adult world. I don't know him or his family, don't know what he will be or what he thinks he will achieve. A lot have fathers in trades and learn their way through to doing the same. I don't know. Could be he'll be this way for life, seeking out the weak to talk down and feel better.

There's no way of knowing, just figuring what's more likely to happen.

I look at him, and see his eyes dart to my mother. She is closer but not hunting us down. She seems to be trying to join a group, or walk as far away from home as she can in a straight line across the town. She has come down the concrete steps from our street above. Blood like breadcrumbs trace her way back.

Mark stares back but his eyes change. I don't know what I am doing, don't know what face is showing. I'm bored of him, and his words and his stupidity. I'm bored of kids just looking at me like I chose this, that I buy into all of this, that I want this to be me and my life. I want him to swing, I want him to feel anger at me, be scared I'll come back with anger. I don't know how to do that, don't know anything at all. Mark looks away as if I have stared him down. He looks back at my mother, shakes his head and runs.

16.45 p.m.

The field of people are scattered. My mother in a vacuum where people had been. She walks in a shuffle like an old man not ready to give up on movement. Blood is dripping from her hand, and her pale clothes, not clean but no one caring as they are spoiled in blood. Splatters and wipes and her face the same. I look around and see them watching as they walk backwards away. They know at distance they are safe. They are watching me too. They are always watching me.

I'm scared, it would be strange for me not to shake, not to find breathing hard. My heart is pounding and my body is telling me to run. I step toward her, not confident nor stupid enough to get within range for her to lash out.

"Mum," I say.

I'm not using a soft voice of concern and care, I wouldn't know how, not with her. Not any more. My voice is how I talk when she is gone from most of reality and needing to be shown where to go, where her bedroom is, where the stairs have always been. It isn't brutal, it's a way to break through the cloud she walks in when she has passed her limit of self-awareness.

She smiles but doesn't look at me, her eyes are rolling and covering every part of the images in front of her. I don't think she sees anything, I don't think she understands the world.

"Mum," I say again, louder, firmer, and her smile fades.

She stops shuffling and turns her face to me. Her eyes stop moving, she focuses in.

"You see this," she says, holding the hand she is using to crush a blade. "This was for you. Not me. Not Quinn. For you."

She steps toward me, but not with the intention of coming. It is a fake-out, a means to make me flinch. And I do, I step back quickly, and she doesn't take a step. She laughs at me, at what she thinks a coward does, at the power she thinks she holds.

"You never could, could you? Never could stand up," she says.

The blood is streaming from her hand, a long thin line like a kitchen tap not turned quite shut.

I have nothing to say, nothing I want to know. I should ask what happened, what is going on. But I don't because I don't care. I'm thinking other things. I'm thinking of the end. The blood could all be hers, probably is. But it could be Quinn's. A squabble, a reaction, a knife at hand and a decision made in the moment high on alcohol and anger. I don't know. But I understand I don't care, and I can't understand why. There is a history, a bond – there should be something, biology telling me to care, to worry, to try and protect. I feel nothing. I look at her.

"What are you staring at?" she asks. "You, the one that ruined it? What are you looking at?"

I stare more, saying nothing. Making sure there is space.

"You want to know, don't you?" she says. "Come here and I'll tell you."

She smiles and there is blood on her teeth.

"It's all over," she says, and laughs. "All gone. Children. You. Darren. Children. You find something and it goes. Taken away. All gone."

She looks at the knife in her hand and squeezes it again. She doesn't wince, doesn't seem to feel anything.

"You want this?" she asks.

I say nothing, just looking at her.

"Always quiet," she says. "Never one to let me know you are there. Me and you. And all the others."

She laughs again.

"Not going to ask?" she says. "Not want to know?"

I don't move, I don't take my eyes from her. She is moving side-to-side, her feet planted.

"I'm not telling you," she says. "But it is all over. All gone. No more of your hard life. No more for you to worry about. No more chance of you growing up to be a man."

She laughs, and looks down.

"Want to take it?" she asks. "Go on, try and take it."

"Move away," a voice booms.

I know enough to step back before looking up.

Two uniformed police are jogging across the grass. They are making kids who have stayed move away. But their words are for me. My mother sees them too.

"Always coming to tell me off. Never good enough to do it though, were they?" she says.

I step back as the two police arrive. A male and female, all in black. The man has a shaven head of thick red stubble and the woman a short ponytail, squeezed back and held tight. Her hair showing flecks of grey through the blonde highlights.

"Mrs. Greegan?" the female asks.

My mum looks at them and smiles.

"Always so polite," she says. "All false though. None of it real."

"Mrs. Greegan?" the male officer says.

"You know I am," she tells them, looking at me. "And that's my boy."

"We need the knife," the female says.

"Do you now?"

"Drop it on the floor and step away," the female says.

"I don't want to. It's mine," she says, smiling, playing, joking.

The male looks to me, as if me being her son gives me a special power over her actions. I shake my head slowly. He doesn't know me, doesn't know us. He would never ask if he did.

"Supposed to hold it like this, aren't I?" she says, moving the blade out of her palm and grasping the handle.

"We need to speak to you," the female says.

"We are speaking. Billy is our witness."

"Can't do it while you are holding the knife," the man tells her.

"Then we can't do it at all," she replies.

The police look at each other, a way of communicating. Maybe they had a plan, maybe there is only ever one plan. The situation evolves and they know what comes next. They step away from each other, trying to flank my mother.

"I know what you are doing," she says. "So you can stop it."

They don't, they keep on spreading apart and to her sides and she moves her head because she doesn't know where to look, who to be defending against. She chooses the male. She was always going to and they know it.

"Stay away," she says, waving a knife like she is conducting a clarinet.

"We just need you to put it down," the male says. "That's all. Nothing else."

She turns to face him, her lips stretched and her teeth showing. She opens her mouth to speak, but she has no chance for words as the female officer hits her from behind, knocking the knife from her hand, bending her arm up and back behind her. My mum screams, swears, tells them to leave her alone. But the female officer forces my mother down, face into the grass, twisting her arm up, making sure she cannot move. My mother swears again, and doesn't stop. She kicks out, thrashes around, but her strength is nothing and her fitness less. She runs out of breath and energy and the last she retains she uses for words of insult. The male leans in to help, placing handcuffs on my mother's wrists. I watch and my mother watches me as she screams basic threats to two uniforms. Nothing imaginative, nothing she hasn't said before, and nothing the police haven't heard.

They pull her to her feet, my mother helping with the movement as to fight against it would be to break her arm.

The three look at me, the field of people watching, kids with mouths open, the verbal ones talking about what they have seen, adding non-existent detail to a story they all witnessed. I am there, in the centre, present but not a part. Someone who happened to be close, not someone who played a role. But that won't matter, whatever ideas they dream up will be there in word and story and whatever they agree to be true will be what holds as fact for the rest of time.

"We need you to stay here," the female tells me.

I look at her, not speaking, trying to figure what she means.

"Stay here and we'll send someone down," the male says.

They look at me as I stare back.

"Can you understand what we are saying?" the male asks.

"He doesn't understand anything," my mum says. "He won't have understood a thing."

"Just stay here," the female Says.

My mother lifts her head, smiling at me, nothing warm, no humour, a demonic grin of wide-eyes, teeth and blood.

"Go and see," she says. "Go and see the end. Go see the house. Go on. I want you to see. Run."

She starts laughing, and the female starts to speak, but I see the fear, the shock in their faces, the panic of an empty head when quick thought is needed. I take two steps back.

"Just stay here," the male says.

But I have turned, and I am running, sprinting to the steps that lead up from the green to the grey of the concrete. From countryside to estate in a flight of twenty stairs.

I hear the blood pumping in my ears and the cackle blasting from my mother's mouth.

17.00 p.m.

The street, my street, is full. I walk to the top of the steps, and walk through the gap in the low brick wall onto a tarmac path that runs the length of the road. The small grass verge runs as a buffer between it and the parked cars that run the side of the street. An unofficial space in front of everyone's house for the family estate. We have none, although people leave a gap all the same.

I have stopped running, my breath short but my mind fast enough to tell me to approach calmly. Sprinting into the unknown is a risk I don't want. My mother covered in blood, police, a knife, her goading me into coming to look. The last is what scares me most. She told me to come, wanted me to see. But I don't know what, and I don't understand anything. I don't know what is there, don't know why she would want me to watch. It will be because she believes it will cause me harm, but in what way I can't be sure.

There are two marked police cars, parked across the road as if blocking the way. But the street loops round like a large lasso so either side of the barrier has a way out. There are twenty people walking around, forming and breaking groups, talking and communicating. Four are people from the street, the unofficial representatives, the people who think they speak for us all, but speak for no one but their own egos. The rest are police, uniform and not and medics. Two ambulances are parked up close to the gate to my garden. Large and white and designed to be noticed. In a future life they will be hippy campers or a builder's van, but right now they are here to provide comfort and help to those in need. I walk the path on the opposite side of the street, ten houses down from where I live. Behind me the gates open up onto steps that go down on sloping gardens to the front doors of identikit brick boxes that act as houses. The difference on the opposite side is that the gardens slope up. The houses are the same, the inside a layout replicated again and again. Three rooms downstairs, and three plus a bathroom upstairs. The difference in each is the personality of the family. Mine is shrine to mismatched design of those buying for cheap functional rather than beauty.

I walk, watching the people and the movement. There are some neighbours standing around, hypnotised by events, staring from their gardens or the red steps at the base of their front doors. Some smoke, and all just stare. I stop, the front door to my house is open. I have seen two medics walk in, and now I see four walk from the ambulance. Two are carrying a stretcher, nothing on top, a white sheet covering it all but flat. Police talk, or suited men I assume are police talk to each other and them. They watch, as I do, the slow procession up the steps, the medics taking it easy, not rushing, not speaking. Two carry bags like country doctors, leather satchels for stethoscopes and orange glass bottles of pills. The police end their conversation, and break from their group like they have just had their pre-game talk and are ready to kick off.

They splinter into pairs and walk to other front doors, asking people who have not walked away questions about what they have seen, heard and what they know. I cross the road, trying not to be seen. All eyes are on my front door and the police moving around. Some people see me, but the police don't know who I am, and the locals don't care to shout and tell anyone. My neighbour is a man named George, who I have never seen. His wife, Ethel I know. She is old, large and has blue hair, or a watered-down blue. She cares for him, or at least that is what they say. He is always inside, always in bed. Our houses are joined by brick sheds attached to our houses and each other. We have a corridor through from front garden to back. Ours has a locked door, theirs an open space. I walk up their steps, along the front of their house, looking into my garden, seeing the people standing there, some looking at me but seeing nothing they want. The local police are away down the road using their town knowledge to find out any facts they can hear. I walk through the brick corridor, see the open door in the side and the shed they use for storage of things that need to be thrown away. On the other side are steep steps up to gardens above. An almost sheer wall of grass and mud that rises above the level of the first floor. Ours is an overgrown mess of long grass and wild flowers, George's the same. Two men who for different reasons don't look after their land.

I walk up onto his grass area, walk across and over the low wire fence that is rusted and close to collapse and step over. I walk to the edge of our garden that looks across into the rooms upstairs. Mine is on the right, the little box room, the bathroom to the left. The window in the middle is for the landing. I see nothing, no movement at all. I crouch down and move as far forward as I can. I look down into the living room. The curtains are open. There are four men inside, all medics. The glass is splashed with blood, there is a white sheet on the floor, not flat but shaped, a body that is clear. I pull back, not wanting to see. But stop myself and lean forward again. The window splashed from inside, two streaks that have run, and a smeared push of red. I can't see enough, I strain to see further in. A man turns his head left and up and stares at me in the face. He speaks, and another man comes into view. He stares at me too. They shout and I can hear a muffled sound but not their words. I stand and step back. I hear the footsteps below, see the back door open, see men walk out, looking up, looking at me. Three come out, the first telling me not to move, the second starting to take the steps up, the third following as fast as they can.

"Billy," I hear and look and see.

Mr. Hutton is with them, out of breath, not welcomed but there. I stop my movement, watch him and the men coming up the steps.

"Don't run," he says. "It is Okay. We need to talk."

I see the police half-way, hands on thighs as they try and take as many steps in one pace as they can. I watch Mr. hutton, I look behind me, see the low fence into the back garden of the house on the next street. I've stood here, looked at the gardens, seen the pets, the dogs, the tortoise, the rabbits, the long grass and watched local fireworks in November, alone and scared and excited. I hear them, I look at Mr. Hutton again, his face smiling, looking for a connection, looking to make me pause, looking to make me stay. I look at the window, see the blood, remember my mother, look at the body inside. I turn and I run.

The fence is easy, low and not requiring anything more than a high step to clear. I am in the next garden, the back of a house that fronts the street behind ours. The land slopes up but not steep. A dog called Ben runs toward me, barking but I'm not scared, I know him, have patted him and given him scraps over the fence. He reaches me as I run to the corridor on the side of the house, open just like George's. I hear shouts behind me, the police not Hutton. He knows when there is no use to words. Ben jumps up and around me, chasing and playing, wanting to join in and have a friend in the day. I feel his front paws push against me as I run and he bounds up, leaping and pushing himself off my body. I wish I could tell him to slow up the chase but I can't. He is a dog, nice and stupid.

I don't look back, I run for the gap in the small building attached to the side of the house. Ben's owner is there, his name I can't remember. A man who grunts and eats is all he is. I dodge past him and I am through the gap into their front garden and the steps up. I take them and leap the low gate kept closed on a latch. I can't turn left and run as that would take me back to my street. There is a telephone box opposite, red and flaking, next to steps that lead up to the top of the valley, where fields start and a large hill begins. I run up, my legs starting to ache, but I hear nothing behind. I don't stop to check, I keep going. I reach the next street, run the hill that loops round and to the left, get to the top, not running anymore, walking, not even fast. I hear nothing but the usual noises of here. There is a primary school up the road on the right, out of town, away from houses, in the countryside. I turn right, go through a gate, into a field and into a wood, I stop, crouch down, draw in breath, push my head back and swear. I slump down, sit, push my head into my knees. I listen for noises, for people, for anything that isn't right. There are no cars, no footsteps and only branches bending high up in trees. I don't know what is happening. I need to think, need to figure something out. I need to do something other than watch and wait and have it all happen to me.

17.30 p.m.

It is over, I'm not stupid enough to think otherwise. I'm not big enough an idiot to think I am wrong and that there is a way back from this. I have pieces of it all, small and large, but nothing to glue them together, or slot them into a picture. I don't have an image to copy, just thoughts and ideas swirling around in what I want and don't want to be true. Darren on a rampage, my mother in blood and a body, certainly dead in my front-room. It is over, the life I had, the one I never wanted. No explanation I can create has an end other than change. I'm scared, not of what I have seen but of what I don't know in the future. A comfort from knowledge and repetition even though it is something I hate. That life is gone, we, as a family as no more. There is no coming back, nothing I can do here without being the son of the woman in blood. Whoever is dead, Quinn, Darren or someone else, marks my home as a murder scene and the street as slum of hate. We did that, me a part of it all. I lean back, rest against the roots of a tree. I know the area, have come here more as houses pushed previous land into estates. Not many come here as there are better more beautiful walks to be had. Here is wild, the paths only just worn in and not bare of branch because they are not used enough. Bushes of blackberries, and thick nettles and coarse brambles are not the place those in touch with nature crave. I know my way, I created some of the paths, even made a den further in. But that will be gone, it's been a long time since such things were what I wanted my weekends to be.

    I hear them, the feet and the chatter, being quiet but not silent. The cars roll up at the gate I came through. I hear the feet hit mud and the doors open and shut. I hear them speak and I hear Mr. Hutton.

    "Here?" a voice asks.

    "It's where he comes, or at least used to. Was heading this way. No place to turn back but here," Mr. Hutton tells someone.

    I wish I were able to translate sounds. Words written can mean different things to when they are said. I wish I could understand the way he speaks. It isn't his teacher voice of quiet command and confident power. It is different, weaker and quieter. I don't know what that means, maybe they are trying to stay calm, trying not to scare and be scared.

I know the way they will come in, there is only one thin path that I walked minutes before. The wind is blowing, not a gale but enough for rustles to hide movement. I crouch, figuring they don't know the layout, and move low and fast away from their noise in a loop around. I could go further in, deeper and hide, but what for? If I keep going I'll be out in the open on farmland opposite. They think I am here so it is best if I am not. But I don't want to be seen, don't want to talk. I have little time left before I discover what's next, what someone who doesn't care decides what happens to me. A decision on how much I am worth, how much money and effort officials feel they should spend to keep me safe.

I try to concentrate, keeping low and moving away but I see my mother, see the body under a sheet, hear Darren shouting my name. I force them out but they bash back in.

"Billy!" they start shouting.

Not together, not as a unified voice, not counted in and then chanted. Four voices that I can tell, each taking a turn to call me like I am a lost dog. All they are doing is giving their position away. They are spread out, but I can't see them and this is a comfort. It means, in my basic logic that they can't see me. I move away, looping all the same. The town is to my left, and getting closer. The wood stops a hundred metres ahead, thins to a field with high grass and brambles. All the trees gone, or were never there. It slopes down onto the edge of a new estate, a richer one, or at least the prices of the houses say it is that way. All light brown brick, and symmetrically placed white windows, with their geometrically equal front gardens and wooden fencing that has not quite gone to ruin because the houses are still, in the grand scheme of things, new. There is a back alley that separates the rows, a thin space of worn-down mud running the length of the street. If I walk through that, reach the other side, I am on the edge of town, with its alleyways and shortcuts. And if they think I am hiding out up here, there will be no eyes to see me.

    I stay at the edge of the wood, listening and hearing my name called less frequently now. They haven't come in deep, there isn't any way they could without walking in single-file. They are close, although not enough for their shouts to be loud. I crouch down again, move into the field, hoping the grass and brambles cover my moves. It is a time when I think there should be corn growing and I could walk through unnoticed. But that is America and the films they show. I walk quicker than before, the noise not as important. I crouch low, walking like a comedian I have seen on TV who pretends to be going down imaginary steps as he wanders around in circles. My heart is beating fast, I look ahead, not wanting to run but wanting to go fast. There is a break, a small strip of mowed grass before the estate starts. I don't think of concealment, I am far enough away from the wood to have a head-start on any of the adults who could give chase. I make it across and hear nothing of running feet or shouted observations. I hit the alleyway, stand and walk fast.

17.50 p.m.

Town is dead. That time between end of work and the start of the evening. Shops are closed and the owners and employees long since gone. There are people around, some live here in town houses, and old hotels converted to flats, but no one I can see although I know they are there. Empty streets and the wind blowing. I walk the sea-wall, the tide in, hiding a brown beach of ugly sand that is too close to mud. I know what I am doing, I know what I am edging toward. A teacher once told a class I attended that some people have no internal dialogue, they have no conversation, nothing is happening but what they see and hear. There is no debate, no conversation, no back-and-forth in constant questioning, no argument and no ridicule over what you did and what you are doing. I wish sometimes I were one of them, no narrator, an inconsistent one too, describing my day and passing judgement on me. I guess that's what some of those people who think they are talking to God mistake it all for. The voice inside their head not recognised as their own and so it must be the words and opinion of a higher being or a spirit or the devil. I don't know. But I wish mine could switch off and be silent.

The loudest noise is the sound of sea hitting the defensive wall on the promenade and the screech of seagulls in the air. I hate them, like most do around here. Those big, ugly birds who snap into aggressive defence when trapped or feeling in danger. They are everywhere and they do not hide. They make themselves loud and clear and demand attention. I avoid the high street with its closed shops, no gratings or bars, only glass fronts to show what lies inside. How they stay open I don't know, there are not enough people with active incomes to spend their spare money here and anyone wanting to splash some earnings would go to the city where there is choice beyond the mundane.

I don't know what I am doing other than staying away from what lies ahead. I need to stop moving, to stay still and think. My flight from whatever it is that happened was my self-preservation kicking in, just like I'd run from any danger, any possible ill that could happen. But I have distance now, physically at least from whatever is happening to me. I will return, go back and find out but when I am ready, when I decide, when I want, not based on the decision of others who know nothing and want nothing from me but quiet.

I walk the edge of town, behind main streets, past the backdoor to a pub called the Brass Monkey. It is a dive, cheap and nasty, and full of men on their way home from work. Smoke billows out from windows and doors, pool balls smack together and laughter follows the smack of a shot but I can't understand the words. There are other pubs too, but this is the one where most go as a tradition of easing down after physical work. Vans and cars are parked nearby and driving laws will be broken sometime, but not as much as they were, not as much as ten years ago when I was little. Pub carparks were full of cars ready to be driven home slowly and not safely. Laws change and people adapt and the bending of rules is in constant pressure.

Quinn never drank here, he wouldn't dare. He didn't work, had no connection with these men and would have been beaten physically by many who dislike the fact he sponges from the state. I guess they wouldn't like me through association, the kid of a man who does nothing to live is hardly better than that man at all.

I keep walking, away from main streets hearing nothing but the background noises of a seaside town that has shut-down but for those who need alcohol to return home. I head toward the jubilee shelter on the seafront for the reason it will be empty, has a bench and roof and a view of the waves coming in. I don't have to cut through town to get there, I could edge all the way, behind shops and through narrow alleyways that would once have been important but are now just there to hold bins and provide a way out if there were a massive fire. But I'm tired of hiding, tired of sneaking around, tired of running. I walk down a street that leads to the centre, where there is a square with a fountain that doesn't work, and benches and telephone boxes and public toilets. It isn't pretty, just a functional central hub to a town that is decaying from the inside out and the outside in. There is nothing here for anyone, least of all me.

I hear his voice and know it isn't him under the sheet at home.

Darren is talking, his voice rising but he is holding back what he wants to say, trying for peace and de-escalation. I try to edge back into shadow but there is none so I move to a granite wall of a bank on the corner, leaning into its rough edge, watching my step-brother talk.

"I came to explain," Darren says.

He is talking to a young man named Gareth whose father is a name around here. A chairman of the Football club, a man on the council, a man who builds and runs a firm that monopolises construction around here. There is nothing illegal about what he does, but it isn't a business built on ethics. Darren works for them.

"You did nothing of the sort," Gareth tells him. "You just came to lie and harass. We know you."

"Something came up," Darren says.

"Drugs came up. Your eyes are still shot," Gareth tells him.

Darren doesn't deny it, why would he?

"I tried to phone in," Darren says.

"Don't lie. You don't care about work, you just want the easy money."

Darren is there, talking to a man who thinks he is more important than he deserves. A young man with a father who has made it as big as you can around here. And his son has breezed into a position of power because he will at sometime become the man that runs it all. He holds the power, holds the ear of the man who pays and employs. He says what he wants and has as much money as he needs because it was all there for him from whenever he started to see the world.

"You're done, Darren," Gareth says. "I told the old man not to employ you, told him who you are, told him you'd mess up, and here we are. Just as I said it would happen."

"It was a day," Darren says. "I came down to apologise. "

"Then why were you speaking to Tracey?" Gareth asks.

"I wanted to know something, nothing important."

"What were you doing to Tracey?" Gareth asks.

"I asked her a question. That was it," Darren says.

Without this power of payment over him, Gareth would have been dropped a minute ago. Darren is holding his peace.

I see more movement.

I look behind and there are others coming, stepping out of a pub on the square. The White Hart, which claims to be a hotel but is nothing of the sort. A place with a cellar big enough to be called a venue, and a pub upstairs that tries to be posh but is just a place for the people who drink but do not work with their hands.

A woman is walking down the street to Gareth and Darren, a young girl, a year above me at school. She looks like she has spent the last year experimenting with growing up in pubs and with men like the man talking Darren down. She is about as pretty as you can get around here and not quite reached the age when pub life takes the fresh edge and adds the size. The childish dimensions vanish into adult bulk. But she is not alone, she is being followed by four other men of the same age as Gareth. I guess they are his crew, or group. They are dressed smart, like they work in an office. It isn't that going-out smart, not something to wear on a big session out, it is an attempt to look like their businessman dad smart. Chinos and shirts and loafers.

Gareth sees them and so does Darren, a group to add power and confidence to Gareth's actions and words.

Gareth steps up close, places his mouth next to Darren's right ear. He whispers, at least I guess he does, saying something quietly so no one but those two hear.

He steps back and smiles and I see the struggle in Darren's face, I see his eyes start to well and while in many that would mean a sadness, to Darren it means shame and his only way is violence.

Darren balls his fists, and tenses up, ready to confront. He nods, little nods and Gareth stands up close smiling into his face believing his family power is a protective barrier against any type of pain.

"Not saying anything, Darren?" Gareth asks.

Darren smiles and his shoulders relax, as if he has seen the answer and the frustration has gone. He knows he can't remedy and get back what he knows he has lost.

"If I hit you, you'll just run to your dad and bleat some bull and be the little coward you are. You know he doesn't think nothing of you, don't you? The only way you got ahead is off him giving you an office to keep you away from the men."

Gareth smiles, nodding away, wanting him to say more.

"On the sites," Darren tells him, "all those men you think you employ, think have some respect for you, they don't. They think you are a little kid with no balls and no brains. Daddy's little fool walking around pretending to be the man."

Gareth doesn't smile, he stares like he has learned from watching actual men.

"You aren't working for us anymore," he says.

Darren nods because he knew that moment had already come.

"If it means having to pretend you are something other than a little pathetic joke, I don't want it."

Gareth smiles now, nods, looks to his friends that have stayed at a distance to watch. He turns back to Darren, nodding all the time as if he agrees. Darren stares him in the eyes, nodding too, raising his eyebrows because he asked for the fight and he is waiting for Gareth's answer.

Gareth steps back, not hiding his anger. He steps forward and pushes Darren in the chest with full force, both hands, palms smacking against Darren's chest and Darren takes two steps back and smiles even wider.

The group of men from the pub start to move forward, slow steps but edging closer.

"You taking us all?" Gareth asks.

Darren looks to the men and back to Gareth and smiles.

"Want to know what I was asking Tracey?" Darren asks.

Darren leans forward, puts his mouth next to Gareth's ear and whispers his own words. He steps back and Gareth can't hold it all in. He swings, a right hand, a wide arc. Darren ducks, makes a shuffle to his left, turning his body and loading his right hand. He sets his feet and swings, smacking Gareth under his ribs on the right side. The boys start running as Darren looks down and smiles at Gareth who has fallen forward onto his knees. Darren watches the boys, pauses, thinking of taking the beating, but turns and runs.

I see Darren is sprinting, a man chasing behind, closing the distance, catching up quick. The man behind leaps forward and tackles Darren from behind. They fall together and slide on tarmac.

They are scrambling on the pavement outside a bakery where they display iced-buns in the window.

Darren swears, telling the man to get off.

"What the hell are you doing?" Darren shouts.

"Stopping you," he says.

The man is on top, sitting down on Darren's chest, as he struggles to hold Darren's wrists as Darren tries to break free. The energy they are using is pretty intense and neither is trained for the exercise.

"Get off me," Darren shouts.

The guy who chased Darren down is young, I don't know him.

Darren moves quick, throwing his hands forward and his weight to his left. The guy on top swings to the side and Darren pulls him down by the collar now his hands are free. The guy's shoulder slams into the concrete and Darren is up and over him immediately.

"What did you ask Tracey?" the guy on the floor says.

"Tracey," Darren shouts, "tell this idiot what happened."

"He asked me if I had seen someone, I said no," she says in a whine that is looking to be deep.

"See?" Darren says. "I wasn't trying it on, I wasn't being aggressive, I wasn't doing anything that you think in your head was going on. You get that?"

"You didn't come in for work though, did you?" the boy says.

"That isn't why you are trying to fight me," Darren tells him.

"You know nothing," the boy says, and Darren leans over him.

"You are on the floor, you brought this not me. I could hit you now," Darren tells him

"And they would jump you," the guy on the floor says.

Darren doesn't let go. He turns his head and looks at the boys walking toward him, Gareth with them, walking gingerly, slower than before, not wanting to catch him up. Tracey has stopped near him, smart enough to be a distance beyond Darren's reach.

"You can't do it on your own, can you? Always someone else," Darren says.

"That's because I have friends, and you are hated," the kid on the floor says.

"Isn't that the truth."

"Let him go," Tracey tells Darren, and he does and steps away, looking at his clothes, putting his top straight. He looks around at the street and sees me. I don't think he understands at first, the fact it is me doesn't register.

The boy on the floor stands.

"You think you can work for us again?" he says.

"That's for his dad to decide," Darren tells him.

"You don't think he'll listen to Gareth? He'll tell him what we know. You blew off work to get out of your head and then letch on his girlfriend."

"She is about twelve," Darren tells him.

"I'm eighteen," Tracey corrects.

Darren answers but looks only at Gareth.

"No, you aren't, not yet. And Gareth there is twenty-four."

The four men start to walk him down.

"Want to do it?" Darren asks. "No assistance? Didn't think so. Your father knows you are a coward."

"At least he isn't a drunk," Gareth says.

"Quinn?" Darren asks. "He is. A monumental waste of space."

"And you inherited that."

"Too early to tell and too late to change," Darren says.

Gareth smiles.

Darren looks at me, back at the boys, and then back to me.

The four boys start to edge closer and Darren starts to back away. The four boys look to each other and start to sprint, Darren turns and runs too, toward me, fast and the boys chasing don't seem to be keen on catching up quickly.

I watch Darren sprint toward me, no sign of stopping. He slows, looking over his shoulder, then looking at me.

"Don't go home," he shouts. "Just don't go."

And he is past, sprinting away down the main street, toward the edge of town and the docks. And four boys are running after him. Gareth and Tracey have slowed to a walk, Gareth holding his side.

They reach where I am stood and stare at me, standing still. I smile back, refusing to look down at the floor. Staring into his eyes expecting to be slapped as revenge on Darren.

"That's his little brother," Tracey says.

Gareth looks at me, looking down, not smiling, trying to intimidate because I am a little kid in comparison.

"You another one of him?" he asks.

"I'm just me. What did you tell him?" I ask.

He smiles at this.

"I told him the truth. I told him who he is."

"And you two? Who the fuck are you?" I ask.

He lashes out with his left hand, an open slap but he misses as I duck and move in the way Darren had just done, shuffling and setting my feet only I don't throw a punch. Gareth has seen and he is smart enough not to try. He'd win, I know that. But he doesn't, and being dropped by Darren is one thing, being humiliated by me is another. The risk, reward isn't there.

"A real man you are," I tell him.

"Your brother is a druggy coward," Tracey tells me.

"He pushed you off because you tried to take an eye."

"You still don't hit women," she says.

"He didn't touch you, and you're an idiot" I tell her.

"And you are a Greegan," Gareth says.

I stare and smile, looking into his eyes.

"I'm me, and you are you. You aren't your dad no matter what act you pull. Call yourself what you want, but I can see you. And you aren't no better. Neither of you."

18.10 p.m.

Darren is alive and not the person under the sheet. But I knew it wasn't, knew it couldn't be. Quinn was the only answer that would fit. My mother with a knife and covered in blood. I didn't see Quinn when I was there and no way he was hiding. My mother with a knife and blood. A dead man in the house but Darren running wild all day. It doesn't make any sense to me, nothing at all. Darren will know, he told me not to go home. He knows, or has heard or has seen, or was there. Something made him tell me. He had a chance to do or say anything. I expected a cuff on the head, or an insult or a silent stare. But he told me not to go home. He knows, he has seen. He can tell me. He has answers.

He will be hiding now, of that I am certain. He looked drained, the high and anxiety of this morning gone. He shouldn't be here, shouldn't be doing any of this. But I need to know. I don't want to hold back and wait, let someone tell me what has happened, someone who will have changed the story, or left out what I need to know because they decide it isn't worth telling.

I hear voices, I realise it is the boys looking without enthusiasm. If Darren was out and easily seen they would chase him down again. But they are making no effort to seek him out in places they would have to look. Gareth and Tracey are with them, walking around, winding it down, ready to head back to the pub or home. The anger and excitement now just boredom and the realisation they were losers when they outnumbered. I have climbed up steps to a balcony for offices. The windows and frames and walls have not been cleaned in years and are thick with gunge, an accumulation of dirt and water over time. I watch the boys as they wander back into a group and chat. They have nothing left to enjoy. They have tried and what is the point of looking for someone they hate. They will tell each other he is dead next time they meet, or some such school boy nonsense. They will all be happy that no one is telling the reality as it is. I watch them walk away, starting to joke and smile.

I hate the docks. They smell, there are rats, big rats. I've seen them, up close and they don't seem scared of humans. You can hear them when things are quiet. Darren brought me down here when he was still at school and still too young to be feared. I don't think it was to scare me, although it did. A playground of danger and no security to keep us off. Until not long ago the play park near our home had a disused tractor as a climbing frame. But the council took it away because it was unsafe for us even though it hadn't been unsafe for previous generations.

I guess Darren is in here somewhere within the warren of crates and cargo holds and sacks and grain. There is no point calling his name, he won't appear to say hello like we are old-time buddies and this has all been a prank. He is hiding, and he'll stay still, not move on because he needs time to think and decide what to do.

I think of when we came down and he took me to the end of the dock where thick wood held everything up, and there was a layer of slimy green algae covering steps that led down to wet sand below. A criss-cross of beams where some people fished, and Darren went down and showed me crabs, and how they were easy to catch, and then release them back. Two kids with a bucket and a stick with a net catching animals to see who could get the biggest and then throw them away and go home. It made no sense as an activity other than something to do. And we did it, but not enough. Just once is all I remember. There were thick ropes too heavy to move and old tyres tied up on the side of the dock to soften the impact of boat on wood. There were warnings all over, at school and in town about the place not being a playground. But there were parts you could go. There had been a pub there, right up on the dock until a few years ago. It was gone now because office and storage space made more money and no one wants workers to drink. And families didn't want alcohol while inhaling the smells of a working port. That was when Darren had learned of the places to play, and places to hide, back when Quinn would seek pick up work and then spend the cash-in-hand on drinks before he got home. Seems like a lifetime ago, and for Quinn I guess it was.

I weave through the new part, the metal frames and cranes to lift loads from boats. The new storage warehouse with bright red roller doors. The building built where there had been space to leave commodities, and now they wanted a roof and a lock and key to stop thieves and decay. The old was going and the new had come in. I walked the length of the dock, reaching the part where the pub had stood, looking further down to where the dock remained the old type of thick chunky log. I see the gap in the rail, the top of the wooden ladder down, try to remember how long ago it was when I had been here last. I have no idea, no idea at all.

I turn and look around and see and hear nothing on the dock. I grab the posts at the top of the steps as I have my back to the water and move my right leg out and down until it feels safe on a rung that is dry as the water never comes this high. Lower down is where the danger is as years of being submerged twice a day has left slime and algae and water damage.

I hear the water and look down to see a small patch of mud and green and sand. I take careful steps and place my right foot onto the ground. I look to my left and I see him, Darren, sat leaning back on wet wood, his head bowed forward and a cigarette, rolled by his hand, dangling from the fingers of his left fist.

He appears to be lost, I think he is crying, or has been and this is the end of what he thinks he needs to go through. He sniffs and I am sure. He wipes his face with his right hand, head bowed at all times.

"Darren?" I ask, quietly.

He moves fast, jerking up and on his feet, ready to charge, but he sees it is me. He doesn't relax but his anger goes no higher. He stares at me and his eyes are red and puffy.

We stand and look at each other, me not expecting him and he not expecting me. It was a long shot, I thought, but here he is. He starts to relax, looking and trying to hear others.

"You alone?" he asks.

I nod.

"Gareth and those, they about?"

I shake my head.

"They're gone. Back to the pub I think," I tell him.

He takes a deep breath without smoke, and looks up to the underside of the wooden pontoon.

He breathes out loud and slow, puffing his cheeks, turning off the attention for a moment to relax. He rubs his face again and takes a drag on his cigarette. He turns to me.

"What are you doing here?" he asks. "You keep following me about. What's going on?"

"You are the one that is following," I say.

He looks at me as if I am stupid, as if what I said doesn't make sense or is a riddle. He starts to smile as he figures things out, and his smile widens again and I see the happiness at whatever he has going through his mind.

"I guess I am, of sorts," he says.

He stays where he is, leaning back against the post, smoking his cigarette down to the end, pulling pieces of tobacco from his lips when his saliva makes them stick to his tongue. He throws it on the sand and it fizzles out in the damp but he steps on it all the same and twists his foot so it is buried. He stares at where it can still be seen.

"You remember when we first met?" Darren asks.

I think about this and I'm not sure I do. I think there was a moment when we crossed paths before I knew of my mother and Quinn. Maybe they set it up and maybe they didn't. Maybe things just happen and there is nothing you can do. But he means when we moved in, or rather they moved in with us to our council house that had been only ours.

"I remember no one being happy," I say, and it is the truth. There just seemed so much anger.

Darren smiles a little, as sad as a smile can be.

"We were Okay, for a time. We had moments, right?" he says.

I smile because I didn't think he had ever felt that way.

"We did some cool stuff," he says. "I can remember that."

He looks away into the distance but I think he wants to see the past.

"You remember digging a hole for action man and letting him sleep out at night?" he asks.

I laugh because I do.

"What weird shit is that about?" he says.

"We were Just being kids, Darren," I say.

He turns to look at me and sniffs.

"You ever seen an adult?" he asks.

I guess I don't know what that means. Have you seen an adult? In years without doubt and at school teachers are that way, or at least should be. But I don't know them away from education. Maybe they are all childish too. I don't think I'm never finding out.

"Why are you running around?" I ask.

He turns to me slowly, rubbing the back of his head. He looks up and squints although he can see me perfectly.

"I have to speak to someone," he says. "I need to find them. I've tried but it isn't happening."

And he looks away again, out at the water, and the way it is thinning and drifting away.

"Do they want to speak to you?" I ask.

"I don't know. I think so. I hope so. I have to find out."

"I can help."

He shakes his head.

"No, you can't, Billy. I'm sorry. It has all changed. I just don't know into what yet."

"Tell me what happened," I say.

He looks down at the wet sand and mud, shaking his head.

"There is nothing to tell."

But I can't accept that, I can't walk away, can't just say, oh well, okay. If that is it then I will; accept.

I let time pass and he makes no move to go. He starts to roll another cigarette but hives up and just throws it all away, tobacco and paper, and it blows in all directions.

"You brought me down here years ago," I say.

"That how you found me?" Darren asks.

I nod.

"I didn't think you'd remember that," he says.

"Scared me, I remember plenty when I am scared."

Darren laughs at this and nods.

"Quinn saw," Darren tells me. "He said it was mine and his and no one else. Clipped me for it. Bringing you down here. But it was his and mine. He'd come down here for some reason, certainly not me, and I'd been there too. Man, I don't remember. I thought it was cool. Different. Weird. I liked it. I come back a lot. Because it is just mine. Nothing to do with Quinn."

He swallows, and looks around thinking it might be the last time, at least that's what I'd be thinking if I were him.

"No one ever around. Not at this time," Darren says.

I can feel how he is thinking, he has slumped into a downer after a long high. I see it, or saw it in Quinn and my mum, that huge dip in energy and excitement, the come down from whatever high they had. Glum and sad, and waiting for something to happen, knowing it will be bad, and wanting out.

"What was that at school today?" I ask.

It takes him a second to process the question, as if connections are not clear. He nods.

"Me being dumb," he says. "I made a bad decision."

"Off your head?" I ask.

He smiles like those trying to hide a pain, closer to a wince than happy.

"Something like that, yeah," he tells me. "Something like that for sure."

He isn't looking at me.

"You afraid?" I ask.

He doesn't want to be, he never has. A kid always trying to show he is brave but for the wrong reasons and to impress the wrong man.

"I got to figure something out," he tells me. He looks at me, really stares. "Do you trust your mum to tell the truth?" he asks.

I am her son, I should be her defender, the person who sees positives, who loves and cares and wants to be someone for her. But that isn't natural, not real, not here and not for me.

"If she wants to save herself, she'll say anything. You know that," I tell him.

He nods.

"I know. I just wanted to hear that you did. I was there Billy. I saw."

"What did you see?"

This is what I want and need to know. Why I am here, I want to tell him. I want to grab him by the neck and demand to be told everything he knows.

He looks at me, opens his mouth and nothing comes but a stutter of sound, vibrations chocking out in his throat. Then he can say nothing more, and I turn to the noise we hear.

There are voices, the banging of sticks against metal containers. There are sirens and there are shouts, and the shouts are from a strong group of people.

They call Darren's name, they shout that they know he is there. I don't know how many, but some are official and some are would-be vigilantes and others are just there because nothing ever happens in this town and when something does it has to involve them. The sirens stop, as cars pull to a halt, police cars and doors opening and thumping shut. They are close because the Port is big, and the Dock is long, but not more than a football field, not the main area. They are close enough for sounds to travel and reach us with volume and ease.

"They are coming for me, Billy. You get that? It doesn't matter what happened or who did what. They are coming for me. They won't ask questions, not in a way to hear my answer, just in a way as to make sure I say the wrong thing and they can twist that stuff to put me away."

"You don't know that," I tell him.

"I've lived that. You think I don't get hurt by this?"

"I don't know what this is."

"Quinn is dead," he tells me, and it is the only thing I know.

"You can't escape, or get away. It just isn't going to happen," I tell him.

They are circling around, feet moving and voices ordering other people to look, and some are just loud and there for the fun. The cars are covering the main way in, because that is from where the sirens came. There are two small exits out, the old main entrance and a side street that used to service the pub. We are trapped and Darren knows it.

"Can you hear dogs?" Darren asks

I try and hear barks and pants but there is nothing there.

"It doesn't sound like it."

"Me neither."

"Are you going to give yourself up?"

Darren looks at me and smiles, a happiness returning to smash away his panic.

"Not to them, not now. No way. Got things to do."

"You can't run forever," I tell him.

"I don't intend to. Nobody ever has. I'll give myself up when it's time. And that isn't right now."

"What are you doing?" I ask.

"Being me," he says.

The tide is going out but it isn't enough for sand and mud to appear along the edge of the dock. A River port whose activity is dictated by the tide. The water is in but has turned and is on its way out. There is no way to edge free to safety. The light is too evident for an escape through swimming. He can hide, but he can't get out, not yet, not without being seen by the masses and not without being stopped by police or local people whose dedication to the law has become something they cherish because excitement and violence may come.

"Darren!" they shout, more than three voices. Again and again as if they are repeating the lines to a film.

"We don't have time," Darren says. "Get going."

"Did you kill Quinn?"

The shouts come again.

"How far away do you think they are?" Darren asks, ignoring my question.

"Close," I say, staring at him, begging with my eyes for an answer.

He nods and taps my shoulder. He crouches and moves fast, the edge of the water, jigging and jumping as the water deepens and his legs get wet. The wall is impossible to climb, it is a drop down to water, a ledge hanging over on struts and then just stone wall where boats lean when waiting their turn, or resting up for the night. I watch him and the water is up to his neck and he is swimming of sorts, and walking too, using the wall as a shield and a means to drag himself along.

It isn't smart but there are no options left. That is his only way out and it isn't a way that will work, not alone. There are none. Police and locals hunting him down and he'll be seen because he can't make it around to the far side fast enough. The people will be here soon, and looking for him. They will see and shout and have people on the other side to pick him up. I watch him and he is trying to glide, not panic, looking ahead and not back, his head above water, his legs working under, like a one-armed doggy paddle with his left hand holding the wall, trying to stay attached. But he is obvious, anyone looking could see.

I have to think, but I don't have time. I am trapped too. But they aren't looking for me, not all of them. Maybe the police have an idea of who I am, and what I could mean to it all. But they are here for Darren, of that I am sure. The word has got around among the men. Police have asked, or Gareth called it in. Darren behaving like a mad man. Tracey could have called it, who knows. But someone has and they are here because that is where they said he ran, and he did. I can stay here, hidden, waiting for them to spot and make their move. I have a chance to remain unnoticed and walk away when their attention is in the water.

But I don't want that and I don't know why.

I walk to the steps and make my way up. I hear the people moving as a line through the docks shouting 'Darren' and talking to each other telling anyone who will listen that they haven't seen him yet.

I reach the top of the steps and move onto the dock. I look around and see no one but I can hear them clearly. They have moved down from the main entrance, no one moving ahead, they have stayed as a line, a wave moving through. No way to pass by without being seen and caught, and the three ways out manned by people who are just there for the fight. I walk to the alley where the pub used to be. A small lane that let drunks in and out when closing time had been and gone but people wanted more drink. A way out and in that everyone knew but pretended to be secret so no one was caught and no one could claim to have seen a soul. I walk past containers, and hear them close. I shout. "Run, Darren," as loud as I can and their voices and chatter stops. "Run to the alley," I shout again, and I run, slapping my feet down hard on the ground. It shouldn't work, not if anyone thinks. It is like throwing a stone when hiding out and everyone moves to the sound despite it not being anything that could happen naturally.

    I don't know why I'm doing it, no idea at all. I will think soon about the reasons but right now I am just doing. I make as much noise as I can and the brains of some, if not most of the people looking through the dock kick into gear like they have cracked a puzzle that will win them millions. They buy it, or enough of them do, and the line breaks and people run because they want to be the one to catch him or the best possible witness. I run and shout, "No, Darren, this way," as I dart for the alley. I look down and see the gate at the end. Someone has closed it. The spikes on top bent at angles so no one would try to climb. I see no people, no guards. I run and hear people coming after but they are slowing and grouping because they know whoever is here is trapped. The building close in on either side, black from dirt and tall and sheer, a small extension on my left that houses a door and an entrance. A two-door way in, enter a small room, close the entrance behind you and then walk on through to the main building. I run at it and jump, my feet hitting the ledge of the window, and I push myself up and reach out my hands grabbing the roof and the felt covering. I pull and scramble my feet against glass and brick and move higher, throwing my hand over the flat roof, gaining traction on the rough surface, those little stones stuck in thick black gunk giving me enough hold to scramble on up.

"That isn't Darren," I hear someone shout.

I look back and a group of four men are staring at me as I stand on top of an extension.

"Have you found him?" someone I can't see shouts.

"Some other kid."

"It's his little brother."

"Get him then," the voice tells them.

They start to move down the alley.

"Run, Darren," I shout.

I smile too because I have no idea what Darren must think if he is hearing me shout random instructions to the air.

The four men come down the alley. There is a drain pipe, one made of plastic and clipped to the wall every metre with a bracket. It feels wet and slippery, but I place my hands behind it and my feet on the wall and move up, walking like batman in the old 60s shows. I go three metres and am at the roof. I reach and grab at guttering, and swing myself up and over. The edge is flat, full of water and leaves, a metre wide with the slope going up, shallow and long as the peak meets tens of metres away from me. I walk the edge, looking down, looking to see what I remember should be there. And it is. It is a drop, from up here more than I think it is. A drop down to a level, metal platform at the top of zig-zagging stairs. The bottom is gated off, so no one can come in, but coming down I can jump the last flight and be on the road and away.

    "He's up there," I hear a voice shout. But I don't look, I am building courage to make the leap. I shuffle to the edge, lean my stomach on the low wall, move my right leg, then left leg over the edge and hang down as far as I can. I don't let go because my courage leaves me. But I can't hold on forever and my strength goes, my fingers straightening and I drop fast and hard, landing on my feet but my knees buckling and I fall onto my side the metal ringing like a bell. I stand, slowly checking if everything is alright. I run down the steps, get to the first floor, as close to the ground as I can. Lean out and over the railings, shimmy down as fast as I can, drop the last metre, land and crouch, look around, see no one and run across the road, through an empty carpark and into the alley leading to the houses beyond. I stop when hidden, listening for voices and steps and running. But all I hear is my breath, and my heart and my laugh.

19.00 p.m.

I know what I am doing, and I can hear my silent voice telling me: Just do it, get it over with, don't pretend you just happen on the place. But it is better that than trying to figure what I have seen and what has happened and what comes next. My mother isn't going home, not for a while, not to look after me. She might have killed, certainly looked like she had and that means she is gone for good. I don't know how that makes me feel, I don't know how that should make me be. I am an after-thought. She has to be taken away, punished or looked after, or something. That leaves me alone. I can't look after a house. I don't have a job and I don't have a skill and I'm too old to go through a system that would end when I am legally an adult and the conclusions and decisions made are too late in coming. I wonder if they will let me take stuff from my room. I wonder if I will ever sleep there again.

The cliff sticks out into the sea, and even at low tide there is still no way of walking around. The sea is deep, the waves powerful and the current strong. I don't doubt in the past people have swum, but I don't doubt people have died trying. I have no time left, not as it was and all the time I need to see what a future I have. I walk up the hill, hearing nothing, looking for an excuse to run and back away. But none comes and I reach the smuggler's entrance, I look in and see the tunnel get dark and bend, and I smell the sea and algae and salt. A party on the beach that I don't remember being asked to attend. Sarah will be there, no way she stays at home, Serge too, and others, kids who won't know me or who hate me, or who just don't care. I think I prefer those who think nothing of me, those who have no emotion either way on what I am and who I will become. I am nothing to them, and they want to be nothing to me. That is the way of it. I got used to that a long time ago.

    I know I want to see her and I figure there is stupidity in that. She is alive, but pretty dangerous. More than rough edges, a desire to push and see what happens I don't think she can grow out of that. She spoke to me, and listened when I mumbled whatever idiocy came out of my mouth. A fun moment, an adventure, not like those of the famous five from back in the forties or whenever, looking for clues and criminals, although I guess there is that too. I just had someone to hang with, regardless of whether that is healthy or not. I don't want that to be the last moment. I want something else. But not love, or romance or chemical connection, I just want to feel that again. That is weird, I know, but it is all I have. What am I supposed to do? Drink to the end and raise a glass to a life that no longer exists. I've got no time and nothing to do except try and make a memory that lasts better than the ones I have.

    I walk down the tunnel and hear nothing but the sea as if I am walking through the space of a large shell, like I'm a small hermit crab having chosen an oversized new home. I follow the bends and step in thick green slime, and water that that could be fresh or sea. I turn the corners and see the natural light at the end, and I hear the voices, and I know they are there.

There aren't many, maybe fifteen at most, and they aren't in a group but in small pods of people. A fire is burning, illegally I imagine, in the sand. Drift wood and pallets brought in by those who came earlier than me. I am noticed immediately. I don't make it down the steps without three people looking my way, and a point and words exchanged between young male adults, words I can't hear but can guess at. Who is that? Why is he here? Shall we get rid of him? Those three questions follow me around like they are part of me and my life. The answers are never anything I want to know, never full of praise and positivity.

I don't know what to do, how to move or where to look or where to stand or where to hide. I am on the edge of exposed space, at the entrance to a party for kids who made their friends a long time ago. Eyes watch me because this is their space at this time, an unwritten code of conduct giving them free reign for limited hours. If they overstep with noise, damage and fear then the place is taken. No one has ever had this conversation but everyone knows that is the way the process works. Me being here changes their balance. They need to know and I understand that. Anyone new, in any place in this town, is a problem until they show who they are and if they know.

I stand and wait because I don't have the character to brazen out an entrance, wouldn't have the skills to keep going with the fake bravado. I look around, avoiding eye-contact, but searching out red hair and I see it. She hasn't looked, it isn't her role, she wouldn't care. Anyone new just isn't her problem.

I hear my name and look to where the sounds came. Serge is looking at me with an expression I can't translate, not with certainty. A curiosity is there, but I think that is how he watches the world. He doesn't need to look away to think, he stares and watches me as I try not to move. He turns his head away and shouts for Sarah. I watch her, smiling without conviction. She looks to Serge and mouths the word What. Serge points my way and she follows his index finger. There is, I can see and I can understand, a moment when she doesn't recognise or know who I am. I get it, I am not memorable. That is Okay. I feel it though, that burst of embarrassment, something others can't feel, wouldn't understand because they haven't heard the conversations and advice in my own mind. I'm not looking for romance, or a friend, just a moment when the things seem possible. There she is not even recognising who I am anymore.

I look up again and her face has changed, a confusion, but not over who I am, at least I hope, but of why I am there, with them, on a beach. She smiles.

"What are you doing here?" she asks.

She walks over, confident and bouncing, everyone looking, taking eyes from me and she sucks in all the attention she needs. I can't move and I don't want to.

"I don't know," I say. "Nowhere else to go?"

"Home?" she asks.

I don't have one, I think.

"Not the place I want to be right now," I say.

"Me neither. But Jim didn't come back and I got the chance to come."

"Does he know you are here?"

"He will eventually. But I'll maybe be back by then."

"Know what he was doing?"

"Saving the world," she tells me.

I stare at her, my confusion easier to read than hers.

"He got a call at school I heard – he called home to explain, and I listened in - often does, from important people and he rushed off. Happens. He'll come back and not say a word. Be silent for a bit. Happens. Not often but it I've seen it."

I want to say I know the reasons he left, the empathy he has, the person they call in to talk to kids and sometimes parents. He isn't perfect, not universally liked but people listen and always have.

"You're in your school uniform," she says.

I am wearing what I did leaving home this morning, carrying my bag, a kid that made it to school but never made it away again. Or maybe never made it anywhere at all.

What happens when I see Mr. Hutton next? If I ever see him again.

It hits me, there is the chance they think some or all of today is on me. They will want to speak to find out how much I know, how much I was involved, whether there was something that happened, something to give a clue to the blood and death. I will stare and laugh because it is the people I live with, the people they know. What was there? There was them and the way they were and everyone else was just there to annoy. I didn't play any part at all.

"You okay?" Sarah asks. "You look spaced out."

I know I do, I have been caught staring into the distance more than I care to remember over the years. I should try and work on that, try to come up with a way of holding an expression that doesn't give me away.

I turn to her and speak because there is no reason to keep it quiet.

"Something happened," I say, "something I don't think I can walk away from, something I don't know."

I don't know if it is the way I can't hold eye-contact, not that I have ever been good at that, or the way the words don't say anything, just vague implications to something nondescript. She watches me and the smile doesn't hold.

"Bad?" she asks.

I nod.

"I think, maybe, everything has changed," I say, "and I only got to see the last part."

"What are you talking about?" she asks.

I want to tell her but what is there to say? I repulse people when they know nothing of me, so telling them of my mother, of what I saw through my front-room window doesn't make me fascinating it makes me strange, to be avoided more. They will find out, they will know I came here and they will know I am acting weird in the face of pain on my family.

"I shouldn't be here," I say. "I made a mistake. I got to go. Shouldn't have run in the first place."

"Run?" she asks, and the excitement she can't hide.

"It doesn't matter," I say, and mean it. It doesn't matter at all.

"Can you go home?" she asks.

I shake my head and I feel the tears coming, swear silently in my head at my stupidity, at feeling something I can't understand or describe. It can't be sadness, it just can't be. It isn't sad, not in the way of any classic sense. I don't even know if it was Quinn. I'm just making logical conclusions based on what I would like rather than what I know.

"I went, and I ran," I say. "Shit. I got to go."

I feel the tears on my cheeks and what is the point of wiping them away? She has seen them, seen what a weak boy I am. I imagine Quinn watching this, watching me and laughing and saying men don't cry. He never hit me when I shed tears, I guess he never wanted me to stop, not really, especially if no one else was around. He just wanted to revel in how I couldn't handle being upset.

The moment of silence drags out and I am fighting the need to sob.

"You want a beer?" Sarah asks.

I laugh, and feel a bubble of snot.

"A beer?" I ask.

"Why not?" she says. "Nothing else seems to be working. Any preferences?"

"I've never had one, so no, not really," I say.

"Never had a beer?" she asks, her voice going higher than it did.

I shake my head.

"House full of it," I tell her, "and all stock checked and marked. I'd get a hiding if too much evaporated. Just never got round to it. Why would I?"

She looks at me and smiles.

"Yeah, why would you? Stay here and I'll grab one. Keep your head down. Not a good look you crying when we are talking. Drooling is ok."

I think as she moves off to a coolbox in the sand. I don't look around, just down at my feet, hoping no one is looking at me but knowing some are. I shouldn't be here, but where should I be? Comforting a woman who hates me because I exist? Speaking to police to tell them all the nothing I know? Listening to soft voices asking me to open up and speak about what I'm feeling? That is all coming.

"This is what we got," Sarah says, handing me a small glass bottle, top removed.

I take a sip and the bitterness smacks my tongue and then comes back and slaps my throat. She laughs at the face I pull.

"Not sweet then," I say.

She laughs and shakes her head.

"No, and the spirits are worse."

"Worse?"

"Not even close."

"I look forward to it," I say, and sip again despite not liking the sensation.

19.25 p.m.

Sarah has led me away, but I don't know how. She moved and I followed as she expected. She finds a place that is still being hit by the fading sun and sits down. She doesn't ask me to join her but I do and as she knows anyone would.

"You like it here?" she asks.

"On the beach?" I say.

She looks down and laughs.

"The town, the whole place. You grew up here right?"

I've thought about this, about whether I belong. But I don't, and this isn't my home, just a place where through chance I have lived. There is nothing that holds me here other than not being independent enough to leave. There is nothing that would draw me back when I escape.

"I don't think me growing up here is the best way to decide," I say. "I could have grown up anywhere and it would have always been the same."

She looks out at the sea and sips her drink, nodding to herself and she is comfortable with silence.

"What about your brother?" she asks.

"Darren?" I say. "He isn't my brother."

She nods into the distance, agreeing but not really because the answer isn't what she wants because the question wasn't what she wanted to ask.

"You grew up together though," she says. "That is something. You have to know him better than most."

"Not all of it. I haven't known him all my life and certainly not all his."

"Just a lot," she tells me.

I nod and look away to the sea, thinking of the boy or man now, who he was and who he is. There was a time, and there have been others along the way, when he was fun, when he was a kid and we could forget the house and just be young. But they are fleeting memories and maybe not what they actually were at all. They seem bursts of a high, but they are just moments that weren't bad. They seem amazing because they were free of fear, free of Quinn and my mum.

We are sitting far from the fire and people but close enough for anyone watching to know we are part of the group. I keep sipping and liquid sloshes when I remove the bottle from my lips.

"Are you going to tell me?" Sarah asks.

I turn slowly to look at her.

"Is that the reason you are here with me?"

She smiles and nods.

"The main one yeah. I'm nosey. I like to know and there is something going on that has got to you. And I don't think that is easy."

I never understand this, people looking at me and saying I show nothing, no emotion or sign of life. It is just something I learned along the way. Some people learn to push back, keeping people far away and others, like me, just hide it all.

"What about you?" I ask.

"What about me?" she says, looking at me and I watch the understanding coming as she widens her eyes. "Ah, you want to swap stories. I tell you something, you tell me something. Right?"

She is right, I do want that, I think I've wanted that from many people over the years but none ever did. A lot wanted to know about me, wanted to hear a lot of things, would tell me what they wanted to hear. Police sometimes, teachers others, social services too. They all wanted information, wanted my description and my words. No one ever told me about them, never thought I might need something. They all just asked and became angry, bored or absent when I stayed silent.

"Maybe you don't have anything to tell," I say.

She laughs, properly and out loud and some people turn to see the source of amusement and it is me.

"Nice try," she says. "But I'm not going for it. What is mine is mine. And what was is gone."

"But you still act the same way," I say and her smile goes.

She looks ahead for a time, two seconds in total. She turns to me, a smile back but not the same beam.

"I got you a beer. I'll take it off you if you carry on with that."

That should be the end of it, I understand that. A sentence said as light as can be, dressed similar to a joke but stated as a warning that the topic stops here. Don't carry on because this is the line I draw. There is nothing but anger after this.

I'm not playing.

"So this is just one way. You want to know about my life and what has happened. You want me to talk because that'll be fun, or you'll get something out of it. But nothing in return, there is nothing you need to say about you because what? I'm not important, or your life is the one that needs to be locked up forever? That's just bull," I say.

We sit in silence again and I'm ok with that. People are the same. I'm the same. I am just a story people want to hear. It makes them feel better knowing there is someone worse than them.

"My parents are alive," she says.

I don't look at her just as she isn't looking at me. We are sat staring out into space.

"I only know who one of mine is," I tell her. "People guess as a joke, tell me who it is when they know it isn't. Someone else's dad is mine and all that. Funny people everywhere."

We stay silent again. A few seconds at most but enough to understand.

"They took me off them when I was nine. A bit late to get adopted," she says.

"Bounced around a bit?" I ask.

"More than a bit," she says and laughs, I think, at herself.

We sit and sip on beers watching the people at the party get louder and moving with more freedom.

"They got in touch a few years back," she says.

"Did you meet them?"

She nods.

"I went to see them, and they were who they were: two kids in adult bodies. I had vague memories and they were all true. They'd cleaned up but it was still a dump. Wanted me back they said. Wanted us reunited."

I want to ask but know I can't. I have to wait for her to be ready and get there and speak and tell me what she is ok with saying.

"I don't know," she says. "They wanted something, and maybe part of it was me, genuinely me. But we met three times and each was worse than the time before and they stopped making an effort and they showed who they were, which was two people not capable of looking after anyone, especially themselves. Jim told me they had another kid after I left. That one is gone too. From birth. Can you imagine that? A kid taken from you the moment it was born. You have to be pretty messed-up and known for it for someone to swoop in and take a kid away."

I don't want to look at her because I know that type of attention breaks people away from their thoughts. I stare ahead, by my peripheral vision is enough for me to understand she is staring ahead.

"You heard from them again?" I ask.

She doesn't look anywhere else but out to sea.

"Not really. I'm not going to answer so there is no reason to hear. I'm better away from them. I'm not stupid enough to think otherwise."

We sit and watch the water and listen to the chatter and notice the volume rising. I know it is my turn next, to speak and explain, and tell what I have seen today. But I am sat and my mind is racing, and my thoughts are not right and what I am doing is not right. I am sat on a beach being the odd-one-out at a party for people I am not. Once I return to wherever I need to be, wherever I am taken, I am someone else, someone who isn't me. I will have to hide, not show any of who I am.

"Why are you over here?" he asks.

I look up and a boy, or young man depending on what age you want to call the change, is looking down. He has hair on his face but it isn't a beard, not really. Thin and patchy but as good as he can do. His hair long and grown out from a crew cut over eight months or more. All the same length but looking layered because it all starts from different heights.

"Just talking," Sarah says and smiles. "I'll be over later."

She looks away from him and sips her beer and she has told him as kindly as anyone can that she doesn't want him near.

"Are you Darren's brother?" he asks.

"I guess," I tell him.

"You guess? What does that mean? You are or you aren't."

"Then I'm not," I tell him.

"Quinn not your dad?"

"Nope," I say, and look away but from me this means something else.

He is bigger than me but then everyone here is, older too because they have with the exception of me and Sarah all left school in the last couple of years and none have moved away. Some of their friends will have gone to university, others drifted off to nearby towns or already were and have no need to come here now school is over.

Sarah stands and puts herself between me and the guy, who I recognise from being around but whose name I do not know. He is just another big guy who formulated a personality on the back of being something when he was a kid. He is in limbo now, trying to learn to be an adult but using techniques that worked at high school.

"We'll be over in a bit," Sarah says and touches his right arm.

He nearly buys it, nearly moves off, placated with manipulative tricks that women like Sarah make work. The same actions from me would end in a beating. But he can't let go. He looks over her shoulder at me, misunderstanding what she is doing, not realising she is offering nothing.

"What are you doing here anyway? This isn't for you," he tells me. "People like you don't belong here."

"You don't know me," I say, but I don't stand, I look up and see him move toward me but not in step just a lean and Sarah stops him with her palm.

"We'll be over in a minute, Mick," she says.

"Lucky she is here," he tells me.

"Really lucky," I say.

He turns and pushes more and I know that is the only reaction he can pull. I insulted him without insulting, like those jokes when friends laugh even though they are in no way funny. I stand, and Sarah is caught between us. He won't push her out of the way but wants the connection as strange as it is. He pushes up to her and she pushes back. But he isn't using all his force as she would fly away without trouble. He raises his right hand and points at me, extending his arm over her shoulder.

"You aren't your brother," he tells me.

"You aren't the guy she wants," I tell him.

And I got him, I know that and so does he. The truth out there, said in sound that he and she can hear. It wasn't a secret. But he wanted it quiet. The only way to manage his emotion is to lash out.

He pushes Sarah out of the way and she falls and yelps, but it is fake, a last attempt as taking the heat out of Mick and removing the beating that will come. He swings and I duck, and I am worried. The punch was good, short and sharp, no huge wind-up. Mick has fought before and knows what works. I'm smaller and faster and could run, but I can't, not here not now, I wouldn't be able to think back and say I did right. I keep a distance and hope he starts to blow and lose interest, and tire, and settle for one punch I can ride as well as I can and we all walk away feeling better. He throws again, the same punch, all right hand, nothing from the left, which makes things easier. It doesn't look like he'll kick which slows it all down. He throws again, the same hand, the same way, and the same speed. I duck, step out to my left and throw a right in a small arc aiming for just under his ribs. It lands perfectly, all my weight timed to connect, and while he grunts and steps away, there is no damage, no fear, nothing to make him stay away.

He swears, looks down to where I connected and marches forward. He wants to wrestle and choke me out. He doesn't want to be hit again. He reaches out and grabs me because I am too close and he is quicker than I thought. There is not point trying for a test of strength because he wins with ease and can crush. He pulls me in and I twist, and turn and wriggle. Fighting against any hold he tries to pull, I scramble before he can lock in hands or arms. He lifts me, my feet off the ground, chest to chest, and he spins and there is nothing I can do as he whips right, throwing me down into the sand but not releasing his grip. My shoulder and back hit the ground, as his weight hits me, but not full-on, not driving me into a hole, but sliding off my shoulder as his back bends the wrong way. The impact hurts him too and he releases his grip, trying to stand while trying to reach out and grab me again. I scramble away on all fours reaching my feet as I go. I turn, but he is up as well and he runs into me with his head down, wrapping his arms around my thighs. I bend forward as he drives me back and my feet are touching nothing but air. I reach my arms down and around his neck, grab my left elbow with my right hand and squeeze as I pull up. He stands and I am lifted as I hold on, but my legs come up too high and I am flipping over. I release my grip, have no idea of where I am or where I will land. I am falling, I know that. The back of my head hits the ground first and the rest of my body follows, as my legs flip over and I smack down on my back. I take a brief moment to understand where I am, but it is too long as Mick stamps on my shoulder looking, I think, to break my collar bone. His foot slides off my shirt and the sole hits the sand as he forces his shoe down. I wince and yelp at the pain but roll away and scramble to my feet.

He is stood tall, blowing hard, smiling and believing I am done. And I am, as I always have been. I've taken a whack and shown I am weak and have no chance of winning. It is time to walk away and hear voices saying what a waste I am.

I smile back at him and see he is breathing deep but trying to hide the difficulty he has with needing air. I don't look around, seek out inspiration or a kind face that will lead me to safety or show me I am something other than nothing. I bend forward and rest my hands on my knees but I don't need the breath or the rest. I smile, looking down at the sand. I step forward as if off balance but I'm not. I need to be closer and I am as much as I can be. I spring forward, running, head down, screaming noise and not words. I see his feet and his legs as he steps back and I hit his thighs with my left shoulder, pushing through and he moves, steps back, but I have wrapped my arms early around his knees, and am slipping further down. He wobbles and tries to keep balance, but staggers and falls backwards as slow as an object can crash to the floor. He places his hands back and to his sides to cushion the hit. He lands on his arse, sat up, with me scrambling around on his legs. I release my hold and try to stand, and he doesn't know what to do as his position is wrong. I jump forward, throwing my head at his and connecting of sorts but not in the way I imagined. My skull on his cheek, a crack and thud and we swear, and I roll away and stand as he sits there holding his face.

"Idiot," he says, and I don't know if that is at me or himself.

Serge is standing near, saying nothing but only looking, his face stern, angry but trying to show no emotion. The empty look of someone you do not want to fight. No fear, no anxiety, just cold and ready and staring.

"Cut it out," he says, and we look at him, this authority and we say nothing and do not move. "This isn't what we do, Mick. We aren't at school any more."

"The kid asked for it," Mick says.

"So what? He's a kid, and you aren't, and what was the point? You'd kill him. We know that. Man, you even made him fight back and I've never seen that."

"He didn't fight."

"He put you on your arse," Serge tells him.

And the people around laugh and this hurts Mick more than any punch could.

"He got lucky," Mick says.

Serge looks at Sarah and she nods and understands. Serge knows she is Ok. He nods again and she smiles and he shakes his head slightly. Sarah looks down at the floor and I know they have had a conversation about me, have come up with some plan, communicated in the simplest way that no code breaker would ever crack.

Serge grabs Mick firm but friendly by his shirt and lifts him up from the floor.

"You always going to fight?" Serge asks and places a laugh inside the words.

"Says you," Mick tells him.

"You kidding me. When was the last time you saw me fight?"

"Heard you and Darren went at it today," Mick says, and nothing ever happens in secret.

"Nothing happened. Just a talk."

"Not what I heard."

"You heard wrong."

19.50 p.m.

Sarah comes and stands next to me.

"Want to walk?" she asks.

I'm looking at the people, all of them close so they could watch and hear, all of them agreeing with Serge, not because of his words but because of who he is. They don't know his past, or at least don't know much. They know it was difficult and they know who he is now. They listen and are scared enough to stay back.

"Sure," I say.

We take a small bottle of beer each and start walking to where the cliff on the right juts out into the sea.

"What's going on?" she asks.

I don't know why, don't know that I actually want to, but I tell her about the football and my mother.

She walks, slowing us down, not wanting to race ahead, listening and watching me, looking for signs that I am making things up, or exaggerating.

"What?" she asks.

"With a knife, all blood. The police came and I ran," I tell her.

"Ran where?"

"Home."

She has stopped now and is looking at me. She senses there is more because there has to be. She reaches out with her right hand and touches my chest. It is a slow motion angry point but without any menace.

"What did you see, Billy?" she asks.

"A body. Under a sheet."

"Whose body?" she asks, and she has the sound of someone in a horror film waiting for the reveal of the killer.

"Quinn, I think" I say. "I didn't see. But I'm sure it was him."

"Not Darren?" she asks, and I think it strange.

I shake my head and laugh. The day, my life, absurd and stupid and me walking through it like I'm waiting for it all to change without any effort.

"Darren is alive," I tell her. "I spoke to him on the docks."

"What?"

"Long story," I say, smiling because I can't feel any other emotion.

"Tell me," she says, her finger pressing deep into my chest.

She watches me as I talk, making the story as short as I can, just retelling detail and the conversation as best as I can remember. Her face doesn't try to hide anything. A shock and an anger and a fear. I finish with me here and I feel lighter as if I have given some weight away. Only I look at Sarah and see that she carries something I didn't want her to hold.

"Jim was there too?" she asks. "That was the call he got?"

I nod.

"Mr. Hutton was there," I tell her. "I ran away."

She looks around and takes a step away and then back and she looks around, searches out Serge, sees him as he looks at her. His face is worry and she smiles back. She moves from side-to-side, stepping like the sand is hot.

She rubs her head and swears and laughs and stops and looks at me.

"What time is it?" she asks.

I look at her unable to answer. I don't know and the question wasn't one I expected.

"I don't know," I finally say.

"Darren is out and they are looking for him?" she asks. "And Jim is there, and your mum is covered in blood, and you're pretty sure Quinn is dead? Jesus, Billy. Why are you here?"

I look at her, stare into her eyes.

"I've got nowhere else to go. I'm not involved but all those people, all of them, have chosen my life, where I am. Not me. Them. And I'm here, and they can all go to hell."

"And Darren?"

"He's as stuck as me," I say.

Sarah bends forward and screams and Serge looks.

Sarah straightens, her face not angry, only sadness and sorrow showing. I've seen it before and it is all for me.

"Why did you help Darren?" she asks.

"Because nobody helped us," I say.

She forces a smile because I think she believes what is needed.

"Jim is there too?" she asks.

I nod.

She stares at me, waiting for something but I don't know what that is. If I did I would offer it up right now.

"What the hell are you doing, Billy? Are you insane? You left Darren in the water and people hunting whoever down? Your own mother covered in blood? Whose was it? Her own? What is going through your head?"

I stare at her because I don't know. I'm here because I want to be, because other options seemed worse, seemed the end, seemed to be anything but what I wanted to be. I chose this, to be here, chose to come and see her for whatever reasons I don't know. I got nothing right, got nothing at all.

"I helped him," I say.

"Who?"

"Darren."

"You think that?"

"I know that."

Sarah bends forward again as if in pain, as if her stomach is cramped up and on fire. She swears. She stands upright. She stares at me, and shakes her head, wincing with agony but brought on by thoughts rather than nerves.

"I got to go," she says, and swears again as whatever plan she is making in her head is facing obstacles whenever a solution arrives.

She stops and stares at me.

"Don't follow me, just stay here, do what you have to do," she tells me. "Jesus Christ, Billy. None of this is normal."

We all watch her, everyone on the beach, the darkness more, the fire brighter, words exchanged and looks too. Some stare at me, all of them do in turn, eventually. Billy, the kid who caused Sarah to scream. I'm not part of them.

I watch Serge race over to block Sarah's way. He grabs her and she shrugs him off. I watch and don't move like everyone else. I am happy the eyes are not on me. She pushes him away, says something I can't hear and Serge looks to me. Sarah says something else and Serge nods and steps back, letting her go, letting her move, letting her escape from whatever this place has become to her. Serge doesn't watch her go, no one really does but me. She walks fast, her feet twisting in the sand and she is gone into the darkness and I am stood alone with a bottle of beer, away from the people and not part of anything at all. I am fooling myself if I try to believe these people want me here. I turn away from them all. I don't need to be their object of hate. I have made Sarah leave and that, for them is the worst I could do. I look up at the cliffs, and how steep they are, how brown they look. I know it is clay, but it just looks like mud.

I walk to the edge, the cliffs sliding up and away. Parts of the face covered in mesh, a means to stop rocks falling and landslides starting. The mesh doesn't cover it all, just patches where steep, and rocks hang out of the face like someone threw them in years before. I'm trying to see if I can recognise any of what there used to be. A hotel that burned, a hotel with a walkway down to the beach. The bottom is gone, but there is a slab of concrete, framed by thick pillars that was once another tunnel through. All blocked and had been since anyone alive can remember. Maybe it went nowhere, maybe it was fake. But it was there, the top half visible through the clay, the majority hidden behind rock-fall. I look up, and I know I am searching for things to do with my eyes that isn't turning and looking at the party. I am not one of them and never will be and why would I want to be a member of that? They are not me and I am not them. I don't think they are a group of mutual love and respect, they are just a group that tolerate and laugh and talk. They have links through school, work or friends and mostly age. They have interests that cross over in sports and loves and likes. They have common experiences and shared childhoods. I don't have any of what they see as life and none of them need me to be part of theirs. I offer nothing to them, but they offer nothing to me, not as a group.

They are individuals I don't know, and I will never know what they are each genuinely like away from a crowd in which they have a role and means of protection, a way of being part of something that is bigger and safer than them alone. They are a community of sorts and some will drift away, some will realise they have joined something that is not for them, and some will stick to it knowing nothing but the security of familiarity. I snort and laugh at myself for thinking that being here with them makes me part of their whole. It just makes me an invader, a pathogen, not even a parasite because I can take nothing. Their defence is stronger than me and I have already been ejected to the outside looking in. They will remember and see me coming and know that pushing me away is best for their group, best for their safety. I have forced Sarah to go, the one person who let me in and the one person they would care to trust. I am an invader that has taken some of their health, taken away a person they all love and see and imagine being alone in romance. They will not want me near again. They are waiting for me to leave, but rumbling on whether to make me go.

I look around and see the fire and see people stood holding beer and talking. I see the smoke and the flames, and hear voices in conversation and music playing on cassette. They care little I am still here, but that would change were I to get close. The beach and the cliffs are not theirs to rule, but the space they occupy is theirs to police and the stares I get when people look my way are warnings to remain at distance.

The way Sarah spoke, the words she used, the sound they made all tell me what she thinks. I am the crazy little kid who makes bad choices contaminated with the lives of others. She is worried about Jim, and has gone to seek out his safety. She could care that much for another, or she could be scared of losing her safe life with him. I don't know. But she wanted to leave and she didn't want me at all. Another person who sees me as I see myself, a waste. Today, trying to stand up, trying to be part of it all means nothing, a false step and I have nothing to do now but wait. I have nothing to do but kill the last of my time here until I am found or I walk myself into a station and people decide what for me is next.

I look up and see the remains of a concrete step, high up, well above where the biggest waves crash when the tide is in and a storm is flowing. There is green of bushes that choose to grow exposed and in earth that has no guarantee to stay. I place the bottle of beer on the sand, throw my bag over my shoulder, and climb on mesh, aware of the danger signs showing rocks bouncing down and climb, looking to see what history there is left to experience.

The climb is easy, the mesh solid and thick. It is twisted wire to make cables, secured at corners with heavy metal clamps. The way up is not vertical but close enough for me to think that letting go will result in a fall that could not be seen as a tumble. I look down and the sand is only metres away but the distance seems much more when above.

The space on the ground I could cover in six steps, but up here, clinging to cable it is a bone-breaking long way down. I look around and see what I am looking for, further up, to the right, a glimpse of grey and concrete. The point where steps changed direction and came back on themselves while still moving down. I try to remember the photos, always from a distance, always from the water. A man on a boat with an old-fashioned camera taking a shot for publicity. A hotel with a private walkway to a private beach. They say the owners made the tunnel, but this is not something I believe. Maybe they reinforced it, maybe they claimed it, but the tunnel has been there since times of pirates. There are a few more natural ones along the coast, small tunnels up through the face of the natural sea wall, worn out and created over years through weather and movement. But they are blocked on each end with manmade brick and mortar because they wanted no easy route in for enemy soldiers in the Second World War. It seems so strange that a little seaside place like this, so insignificant and small could have been so caught up in what always seemed a battle between cities. The pier held a gun, a single gun, more for show than for defence. A single gun manned by lucky men who stayed at home and didn't find places in foreign fields. A single gun that wouldn't repel even one single boat. My imagination is good but to place myself there in that time is impossible to do with any level of accuracy. Would I be brave and buy in and fight? Or would I hide and declare it not my war? I don't know. I know I wouldn't want to kill or be killed, not for something that meant nothing. To gain a hill or a piece of land, or slow down an advance. My life for that seems an unfair exchange. But I don't know. There were kids like me then as there are now and there will be. Choices are something you only know in the moment. And maybe I am just a coward.

I climb up and across, and see a metal bar, bent and sticking out from the cliff face. I grab it and it bends, the base not in a solid structure, and the length giving it space to move. I climb further and claw my way up onto rotten concrete and stone. A platform covered in dense growth of bushes with thick branches and slick oily green leaves. I smile and sit down, hidden from most. I look around, and see that there are steps going up, steps that are crumbled, and some missing and some hidden by green. I look further up and see where they start, the ruins of a once imposing beautiful building, a place people paid heavy money to come and stay and have a private path to a private beach and breathe in the cleaner air of a sea without traffic. It was this now, a major nothing, something the cliff had mostly taken back, something no one was ever looking to save.

I wish I had brought my beer.

20.45 p.m.

I hear, I look and I see. The people on the beach louder now, more alcohol in systems and the level of relaxation hitting what they came to be. The commotion, me and Sarah and Mick all gone from the present and only something to be added later when talking about what had happened. Right now they are forcing the point of having fun and this means different things to different people. Being loud, shouting jokes, running around, pushing and some just still being cool. I had watch them, hidden from view, hidden from the group and nothing to be checked. I am gone for them, no longer here and no longer someone to care about.

I hear the noise, a small engine, a thump, thump of a low-powered diesel. I have heard the sound countless times because if you grow up here and walk near the river, the sound of small, slow outboard engines become familiar. They sound like mini-tractors, or waterlogged scooters. The old photos show rowers more than you see now. They show the ferry as it was then, which is similar to what it looks like now. One of the first slow engine boats to take people across the river because they built the bridge too far away.

The noise is known but unusual here at this time. The darkness coming in, the water not clear, looking flat and dark and dangerous. Close to the sand it is shallow, but it drops off quick like an underwater ledge. I stare out looking for the source and see the small two-man boat built for transporting people to bigger ships or for old men to find an empty peaceful spot and fish for things they will never catch. It is a river boat out on the sea, following the coast, not going deep and heading for the shore, heading for the fire. This would have been the way of it once, a boat coming in from a ship in the sea, a boat carrying men and contraband, following the fire to safety and the shore, the tunnel ready to transport whatever the imported goods were and without paying tax. But now isn't then, and now the people stare and look just as I do.

I recognise one because of her bright red hair, the other takes me longer because the answer makes no sense. But it is him, it is Darren. The two of them in a boat heading for a party she left and where he would not be welcome. I don't understand and my imagination has been shut down too long for a fantasy description to flood through and explain what I see. The boat heads into shore, the party quietens, they watch and the boat drifts in.

I stand and look at the way I came up here to the platform. It would make sense to climb back the way I came. But I don't, I step out, looking forward and my feet slip away as soon as they touch the clay. I slide on my arse and hands and feet, my bag a cushion and an anchor, dragging me slower than I would fall without. I tumble and bounce and scratch, and catch clothes and skin on branches. I protect my face but fall and roll more. I'm not looking at Darren or the boat, I'm not thinking of why they are here and why they are on a boat. I hit the bottom of the cliff, and roll onto the sand. I am bruised and hurting but I stand, and I see the crowd has moved as one wall of people to the shore. I can't see past them but they are letting no one onto the beach like a tribe watching the first contact with Captain Cook. The noise has lowered and I hear the thump of the engine stop. I run as well as I can on soft surfaces, staggering but not falling forward, rushing toward the crowd.

I push through, people happy to let me go, and no one pushing back because this isn't a concert where the front row is for the super fans, this is a confrontation and the front row is for fighters. I break through and I am standing near Serge and Mick. All eyes are on the water as Darren and Sarah wade toward us through shallow sea.

"That's my dad's boat," Mick shouts as he steps into the water to push Darren.

Serge grabs him by the left shoulder and pulls him back. Mick looks to see who dared touch him and eases up on the anger when he realises who it was.

"Wait," Serge tells him.

"He has stolen my dad's boat."

Serge watches Darren and Sarah. They are wading through the low sea and stepping onto wet sand. The boat is drifting and Mick walks out and grabs a rope from the hull like he has since he was tall enough to be above water.

"What's going on Sarah?" Serge asks, his eyes always on Darren. "And why is he wearing my clothes?"

Darren has changed, he is wearing something new, something I haven't seen before, something that doesn't fit: grey joggers and a matching grey hoodie.

"She said you never wore these," Darren tells him.

"I could have given him something better," Sarah says.

"Tell me what is going on," Serge says.

Darren has seen me and looks my way and smiles.

"I came to speak to Billy," he says. "Nothing more."

"Why the boat?"

"It's complicated, "Sarah tells him.

"I'm smart enough to understand," Serge says.

And Darren tells him, "I don't have time."

Serge stares, confident in his superiority, knowing there is no weapon and no threat. He is in control and they all know Darren needs permission.

"Make some or nothing is happening at all," Serge says. "You've stolen a boat, you turn up with Sarah and you are wearing my old training clothes. Everyone here is ready to make you leave. Speak to me or I let them do what they want."

Darren looks around the crowd, looking into faces and seeing those he has known since a child, known as enemies or at best people who don't care. He smiles as he scans them all. He has fought some, insulted most and repulsed them all. I know he thinks nothing of these people. He doesn't want them as friends, doesn't need to be in their social group, doesn't need them to think highly. I look at me and think of the desire I had to be someone like these, someone I had thought normal. I watch Darren and the smile and contempt he shows for them all, challenging them to say something, knowing any beating they would try, he could smash back and make a mark. And at the worst he could take it all because he had been trained in punishment by his father.

Darren returns his gaze to Serge, a smile and an ease in his face. He feels no fear and sees no danger, just kids who know nothing of him and what he has lived.

"Quinn is dead," Darren says.

Serge nods and looks to Sarah. Sarah shakes her head but I don't know why. It could mean a million things.

"I don't care," Serge tells him.

"They think I did it," Darren says.

"And you didn't?"

Darren shakes his head.

"Who did?" Serge asks.

Darren's smile fades and he looks down at the sand. He moves his head up and down and looks to me.

"I came to speak to Billy," he says.

"Why not the tunnel?" Serge asks.

Darren doesn't take his eyes from me and while his words are to answer Serge, they are for me too. A confirmation or a thanks maybe. But they are for me and whatever he means they sound soft.

"Because a lot of people are looking for me," Darren says.

Serge turns to the tunnel, looking and listening, trying to hear or see something to make him believe. He turns back and looks at Sarah.

"You?" he asks.

The crowd are quiet and listening and unsure.

"I'm just helping," she says.

Serge looks at her, no anger only making her aware he is thinking about what she has done.

"This is the guy?" Serge asks. "The ducking out, the missing school, the meeting and the smoking – because you stink of tobacco when you come back. This is the guy? Really?"

Sarah smiles and nods, but she doesn't look down, she stares ahead and looks at the crowd too. She is challenging them to laugh.

"You are genuinely crazy," Serge tells her.

"You told me that was a good thing," she says and Serge smiles.

"I did, didn't I?"

"I just need to speak to Billy and then I'm gone," Darren says.

"Not in my boat," Mick tells him.

"I haven't damaged it. I borrowed it. I didn't have time to ask permission. I'm sorry. I'll pay you. But there was no way I could get here on foot. The place is steaming. Police and people out looking for me, and I don't think they want me to just give up. A few want a piece and I just need to speak to Billy."

"Why?" I ask.

"To tell you the truth. So you know from me and you don't hear what others say, and lies and what people want to think is true."

Serge reaches out and grabs Darren near the throat but on his grey hoodie.

"Did you kill him?" he asks.

Darren doesn't fight it, he relaxes, no tension at all.

"I wanted to, I didn't get that chance. Spent a lot of time trying to be him, trying to make him proud. How stupid is that? But I didn't kill him, and I won't get my shot at revenge. I won't get to show him. Because words wouldn't matter, telling him anything was a joke."

Serge releases his grip and steps back.

"They'll be here soon enough," Sarah says. "There aren't too many other places to look."

"Did they see you take the boat?" I ask.

Darren looks to me and smiles.

"I don't know, Billy. You're the sneaky one not me."

The crowd don't know what to do. There is a party they want, a fire they have burning and people and drinks they want to touch. But here is Darren, the problem they have known forever.

Serge standing and not fighting like he once would and Sarah, the girl they all love and protect, taking sides with the kid they have all avoided since primary. None of them have any chance of making the choices they want.

But we hear it, the shout and the footsteps. We turn to the tunnel and two kids, a couple, male and female, trying to run but the sand won't help, and shouting. We all turn and try to hear.

"Police," the male shouts.

The girl is laughing and holding a bottle, too big to be beer, and the wrong shape to be wine.

"Police," he shouts again.

I don't know if he knows Darren is here, I don't know if they were off in the tunnel looking for privacy for them or because they are smoking something illegal or that they were just caught up while walking and talking to find out if their connection was real.

The girl is laughing, and staggering about, while the lad is sounding a warning like it is the funniest thing he has seen in weeks.

Darren swears. We hear a boat, maybe two. They aren't fast, the same thump-thump of a small slow two-stroke. I look and I can't see them but they are close, the other side of the cliff edge.

I look around, people standing, some ready to move, others waiting for instruction or a thought and decision to pass through their brain.

"Mick," I say. "Want to take your boat back?"

He looks at me as if I am the dumbest on the beach. Serge looks but his face goes from anger to understanding.

"Pretty sound idea," Serge says. "Get your boat out and back and not involved in any of this."

"I'm not thick," Mick tells them. "You want them two to follow me back to the river."

"You aren't thick," Serge tells him. "Want to do it though?"

Mick looks around, sees the crowd watching.

He laughs. "Why not?" he says.

"Take a beer or two," Serge tells him.

I watch Mick step out to his boat, push the bow and turn it around. I see him step in with the ease of someone who has done this all his life. He pulls on the motor and the engine pops. He sits down, looks back and then slowly moves away. There are shouts from the two boats in the water and we see them, hulls no bigger than Mick's but with three men in each. Mick heads toward them pulling on a beer.

20.55 p.m.

Darren is trapped on the beach, the tunnel the only way out. He knows this and he is smiling.

"Not much time to talk," Darren says.

But he is wrong. There is no time at all.

Men in uniform stream through the tunnel's opening. First come three, ones we know and have seen, those that are based in our town as much as they can be. But they are followed by others, more uniforms and then by those in civilian clothes. Most I recognise, but names I don't know. They will be the righteous, the law-abiding citizens of a small town who think the law belongs to them and their lives, not others like us who don't have their money. They all break the law for financial gain, or to gain jobs, or to simply get home quicker. But those are laws for other people, minor laws that mean nothing, certainly not for them.

They swarm down the steps.

"Get your hood up," I tell Darren.

He does, and Sarah pulls one up and over her head too, hiding the red of her hair, the beacon that would bring them all down.

The crowd of kids splits, all of them running as the police tell them to stand still.

Darren watches it all, smiling, accepting.

"I guess we'll talk some other time," he says.

"I can get you out," I tell him.

They look at me, the group around us, the cool kids who don't run for anyone, and are not carrying anything illegal, and have done nothing wrong.

"Serge, I need a group of us to get up there," I say pointing at where the concrete steps lead up to the foundations of a burned out hotel.

Serge looks at Darren and Sarah and the four kids around. He smiles at me.

"You have no chance," he says.

"Humour me."

We move as voices shout and people tell us to stop, or others to stand still and the confusion and running brings laughter from some. The crowd has split and the police don't know where to go, who to chase down. Darren is crouched, looking small in clothes that are not his, with his head covered like most with hoodies. We move as a group, three people with us because Serge is coming too. We move as one and they are following me as the light from the fire is the brightest part of the landscape. I lead them toward the edge, along the cliff face and I glance to my left and see young people ignoring instructions and demands from police, and pushes and scuffles breaking out between boys who are young men and the older generation who caused their own trouble trying to put them in place. We move and we are being watched, we can't go unnoticed, but we are not heading for the tunnel, not seeming to escape, just moving on the periphery as if scared by the conflict. A group hang by the tunnel's entrance, a group who have declared themselves the last line of defence, but who are all cowards and know they have chosen the spot because no one should get through. Three men, large with faces of outdoor work and alcohol dinners are moving toward us. I recognise the man in front, a man named Daryl who Quinn once said had a cauliflower arse for the amount of times he'd dropped him on it. A man who loves the fight but just isn't good enough to be in one. He is flanked by two friends, who are here for the fun and the commotion and the thrill of being men fighting boys. They are nothing. Serge sees them too, and moves toward them. They meet not far from where we struggle to move across sand. Daryl throws a punch and Serge grabs his sleeves, pushes and pulls and flips him over, positioning himself on top, holding him down and pulling on his arm. His two friends jump on, and Serge is engulfed in people. The three boys with us rush across and the pile on the floor of old and young bodies looks like a school game where no one can inflict pain because no one knows what to do. The three men throw punches but can't wrestle, and the four boys, including Serge, are too fit and too quick and know how to move. Serge is up and on his knees. He throws an elbow down and cracks Daryl's face. Daryl's friends are held by the three boys, none of them saving energy, all flailing and there is nothing worse than trying exercise with a stomach full of beer.

    We move, Sarah, Darren and me. I lead and they follow, trusting because there is no other option. I hit the wire mesh, I start to climb, knowing where to go and how to move and avoiding places I struggled before. I look back and Darren is helping Sarah. But she shrugs him off and swears and he smiles and says sorry. She moves ahead, following me, and Darren behind her. I look back at the commotion on the beach. People on the sand wrestling without knowledge, using strength and energy because holds and efficiency are learned and they have no history. Everyone taken up, the police the only ones standing, the old people of the town realising their age and confidence is misplaced as they suck in air and the conflict fizzles out. I see Serge standing and walking away from Daryl who stays down, his nose bleeding, his head spinning, knowing he has been beaten again, already thinking of how to explain, of how he was the real winner, how the kid was all cheap shot and luck.

No one is looking to where we are, and I make it to the concrete platform, crouch down, up high, behind the green of bushes and the start of trees that will never make it big. Sarah comes up and lies down, breathing hard, and Darren climbs up last, falling down, lying on his back, smiling up and Sarah leaning on an elbow smiling at him.

"Anyone following?" Darren asks.

I look around the beach, people having lost their enthusiasm for the game. The police starting to take control, the people being looked at and questioned while most bend forward hands on knees sucking in breath and trying to remember who they needed to hate for the next few years because of the chaos they had caused.

I lie back, looking up at the sky.

"If they have, they aren't saying," I tell him.

21.30 p.m.

We wait, listening, not speaking, not moving. From above we would look like a peace sign made by humans with our heads almost touching in the middle. I inhale deeply and sit up, looking out at the cove. The fire is still burning, the sand empty, the scrapes and divots in the sand telling a story of fight and rolls and running. The fire is dying down, the spare wood unused and sitting in a heap that no one is going to burn. Everyone has gone, no one has climbed to see us and we are alone on a platform.

"It's empty," I say.

The dark is here, light from faraway flames and the reflection from the moon is all that lets us see something.

"What's going on?" I ask Darren.

He sits up, and rubs his head. Sarah sits up too, watching Darren, looking for something I could never see.

Darren looks at me not wanting to speak, trying to formulate words or ideas in his head, ones he is comfortable with saying, comfortable with letting others know.

"I went back," I say.

He watches me again, not wanting to understand what I am telling him.

"The police and ambulance were there. All over. They chased me when they saw I was there. I ran away. Left them all to it. Quinn dead."

Darren nods as he listens.

"I didn't think he'd make it," Darren says, after a pause when he looked to Sarah.

"He didn't. At least I'm guessing it was Quinn," I say.

"It was him. I saw," Darren tells me.

"My mum too?" I ask. "I saw her. Covered in blood. A knife in her hand, walking around like some lunatic. Everyone saw. The whole estate. All the kids at school. The police took her."

"I didn't touch her," Darren says. "I could have but I didn't."

"Am I supposed to thank you?"

"It was her, Billy. Not me. She did the killing."

"Why should I believe you?"

My mother the killer. The killer of Quinn with a knife from the kitchen.

He has no answer because why would anyone believe him? He was Darren, and that meant he was guilty.

"Why were you there?" I ask.

"I went back to go at Quinn again. I figured he'd have drunk, be drunk, or something else and I'd take a better chance. I wasn't thinking straight. I wasn't thinking at all."

"So you jump work and go home and you just walk in on my mum killing Quinn. Why would she do that?"

"Because of what I said. Because of what I told her."

"Which is what?"

Darren closes up, looks away and stops speaking.

"Just tell him," Sarah says. "It doesn't mean anything. It is true."

"I said something I shouldn't have, or I should have, or I don't know. Quinn didn't deny anything, just laughed at me. Your mum listened though, she read it, saw the truth. Knew the truth. You know, all the hate we get because of who they are, the waste of space and time, the drink and drugs and the words of anger. All that and she doesn't care. But the embarrassment. She flipped. They shouted and I just watched. I didn't get it. Didn't think I was doing anything other than spoiling part of his day."

"You watched?"

"I saw, different thing. I stayed out and ran when it started. The shouts and abuse, the pushes and then she just let go. Stabbed him twice before he even knew. He looked at me, but not long. I ran."

"Then why are they coming for you?"

"Because I was there, because it makes sense that I would do it. It makes sense to come after me because I am the one who should have killed him."

We sit and stay silent for a long time. I hear their breathing and my own. Realise Sarah is there and listening and being part of something in which I didn't know she was involved.

"Why did you come up to school? Why me?"

Darren laughs and Sarah does too.

"He came up for me," she says. "I'm always in isolation. That is just where I should be."

"You looked off your head," I say.

He nods.

"Yeah, I took something I shouldn't have. I wasn't making good choices. So I have drugs in my system and a dead dad. I am not exactly looking innocent."

"Why did we run?" I ask Sarah.

"To get out, to be free. To maybe see Darren. I don't know, it seemed the fun thing to do. It was fun."

"And the reason you were at her house?" I ask.

"The same," Darren says. "I didn't know you were there, didn't think Serge would be either. Just hoped Sarah was."

"Serge kicked your arse," Sarah tells him and laughs just the right side of maniacal.

"He has always been able to kick it. It is just the way it is. I learned that a long time ago."

We sit longer than before, just sit waiting, not knowing what to do, what the plan forward can be, what the future looks to be when we have no chance of vanishing away.

"What's your plan?" I ask. "Run away? Hide?"

Darren stares at me as if I am insane. He smiles.

"There is no plan other than keep out the way until I spoke to Sarah and I spoke to you. I've done that now. And now I don't know."

"And now what?" Sarah asks. "Walk into the police station and give yourself up. They aren't giving you an easy ride. Not after today."

"No one is doing that for you either. You should have stayed out," Darren tells her.

"You aren't involved, you say," I tell him, to stop the argument they are beginning.

"You don't believe me?" Darren asks.

I hear the anger in his voice, the disbelief that I would not trust his words. I think he is being honest, but I think he is telling the truth as he sees it, as he wants it to be.

"You went back to do him damage. You say someone else did it. My mum?" I ask.

These are just softer versions of what the police will ask, if they ask anything at all. My mother will have lied, will have done and said anything to make her way out of whatever danger she has created.

"You saw her," Darren tells me. "What was she doing? What was she like? Because she got Quinn in the neck and the blood was coming and then some. She would have been covered."

"She was," I say, and think of the moment that seems weeks past but is only hours. "Doesn't mean she did it."

Darren leans toward me.

"You are defending her? Telling me I'm guilty."

"I'm not doing anything. Not saying anything."

"That's the problem," Darren says. "People just expecting me to be me. I wanted to hurt him, wanted to hit. I nearly had him in the morning. None of this would be if I had won or just walked away. I just wanted another shot. I messed up, shouldn't have gone back. I should have just worked the day."

That is the truth, but it is the truth of every bad moment. We could all have walked away before it happened, all made a different decision, slowed down, stopped or speeded up. Every second we make decisions and there are hundreds before an incident. What if I hadn't accepted the invite? What if I hadn't driven? What if I had just stayed in bed? Or what if I had just got up? The other choice would have changed the present and you play the other outcome out in full, torturing yourself that just one simple choice the other way would have meant a simple sleep. But it was coming, all of this, at some point. Probably a miracle it hadn't already happened. Quinn being alive, a home with four people who lived but hated. Thinking now, looking at it all, the end was this or something similar. A few more years and maybe it would be me with the knife, Quinn older and weaker and me older and stronger. But that is just a wish that no longer needs to happen.

"Mum will be talking, lying, trying to make a way out for her," I say.

"There is no way out for her," Sarah tells me. "Police aren't stupid, police won't believe. The evidence is what it is. They will have seen it before, know what has happened. There is nothing on Darren except running away. I told you this."

"You know the law, do you?" I ask.

"I know what is right," she says. "And Darren ran from a killing. That is all. Your mum is a murderer, not him."

"He was there," I say. "People will have seen, my mum will have said."

"They aren't going to listen to her," Sarah tells me and I understand how much she thinks of Darren.

We leave the words for a while, all of us thinking, all of us seeing three kids hiding on a cliff waiting for some divine intervention, some way to go back to the normality we hated. There is no answer, not for us, not that involves reality.

"How did you get together," I ask.

Darren laughs.

"Out of my league, right?" he says. "I'm too dumb and too nasty for a girl, is that what you are saying?"

There is no anger, only amusement in the way he is speaking. I guess that is what he figured too, I guess he finds it funny that the girl he has beside him is everything he is and more and that the lucky one is him.

"Sat down there, as it happens," Darren tells me. "Some weird redhead who lives with Serge coming over to find out why everyone hates me. And to steal a cigarette."

"He isn't who you think he is," Sarah says.

"No one ever is," I tell her.

I watch as they cuddle up and it still doesn't work in my mind. What I am seeing is not what should be based on the things I thought I knew.

I think of the possibilities, the future, the immediate and long-term. There is nothing concrete and nothing I can guarantee. I need an easier way to face what is coming, a better chance at being heard.

"You are planning on running forever?" I ask.

Darren moves slowly, lifting his head to look at me through the dark.

"I'm planning on being caught," he says. "I'm just trying to enjoy the wait."

21.45 p.m.

I have thought, with us sat there, waiting and doing nothing. We are waiting for nothing.   Doing nothing. There are possibilities and none of them good.

"Stay here," I say. "I got a way. I think. Something better than just sitting and doing nothing."

"There isn't a way out," Darren says. "So just relax and enjoy the peace."

"I'm not talking about a way out," I tell him. "I'm talking about a smooth way in. We need a voice, someone who they will listen to. Someone you have to speak to and explain."

They look at me and think I'm weird, talking nonsense and trying to sort something that is permanently broken.

"You haven't got anything, Billy," Sarah says, "other than a hope and wish. This is the end."

"Then stay here, stay down by the fire. I'll try and then come back."

"With the police?" Darren asks. "That's going to work out well. I'll take the last night before it all blows up to be alone and happy."

"You aren't happy," I say. "Sure, Sarah is cool, I get that. But you aren't happy. Neither am I. Quinn is dead, and I don't care. That is weird. But I'm not happy. How can we be happy after where we've lived?"

"I find moments," he says, "and this is one. No one around, just me and you two. And that is enough."

"Not forever."

"I'm not looking at forever, I'm looking at now. And right now, despite this, I'm ok."

I am standing, moving weight from foot to foot.

"Just stay OK. I'm not bringing the police. I'm not ruining the night. I'm going to try and make the next step easier. Give me that."

"What's your plan?"

"I don't have a plan. I just have an idea. It might not work, probably won't. But I'm not thinking it through because I don't want to see the bits that don't make sense. I'll leave you two alone, you can cuddle up and whatever. But stay here, or stay by the fire. If it doesn't work I won't come back, won't tell anyone where you are. Okay?"

They look at me and then each other.

"Do whatever it is you think you have to do," Darren says. "It isn't changing anything."

21.55 p.m.

I climb down the way I came up, the fire still burning, providing enough light for me to see the way I want to walk. I look back when I hit the sand and I can't see where we were, I can't see Darren and I can't see Sarah. I walk in a straight line to the tunnel, the sand twisting under my steps, I hear noise and look back and see Darren and Sarah climbing down, helping each other, and I smile at how different they are when together.

The tunnel has lighting, spaced apart, and not fit for purpose. It is dark and I guess deliberately to make people avoid the walk at night. The turns are visible but the shadows large and black. To hide in here is easy, but you will be found as the tunnel is too narrow for anyone to stay alone. I can remember when the bends happen, I can see the steps from the poor light. It is barely better than a dark moon. The walls are wet in most places, the floor too. Everyone from the beach bar Mick came down this tunnel. The beach will be covered in discarded drugs and alcohol. Some will have just walked away and headed for a new place to have something extra with small groups of people they liked. Some will have headed home and some would be sat alone smoking and drinking the beer they don't want to throw away. I have no idea which one Serge would be. But the leader, the one they look to is not someone to be the first to call it a night. Maybe he has gone to tell others of what happened, maybe he is talking about what he saw and heard from Darren and Sarah. But I doubt it. He has some type of code, and he wouldn't want others to do the talking for him. I don't know how he reacts, but I I think walking home and explaining it all is too far from who he is to be a possible option.

I think he would head down to the docks and meet Mick and say thanks and drink a beer and make sure all was good. That's what I think, that's what I want to believe of him. I don't know why that is something he should do, maybe I'd like to think if I had his presence, if I had his power, I would make that choice. But me going down there would just be an insult to a kid who wants nothing to do with me at all. The same actions from different people meaning different things to who sees them.

I know where I am going, and I know I have to remain unseen. I sneak around once I am out of the tunnel, staying close to walls and away from pubs. I walk the smaller streets of dark residential blocks. I walk quickly and quietly and stop and watch as if the house I am staring at might move or run or start to speak.

I stand in the road.

The night is quiet and there are squares of blurred light from windows with curtains drawn. There are noises but it isn't people, a few background cars driving late at night from place to place or from a relative to home. Maybe people who work shifts coming and going. The peace in comparison to the day is large. The darkness too, street lights on to help the few walk dogs, or wander back from pubs. A lot of energy to keep empty spaces lit for the chance that someone might need them. If we turned them all off the place would be black. I watch Hutton's house and there is light inside and movement. I can see from shadows that at least one person is inside, maybe more. But the place feels empty. I should walk up and knock or ring, or find courage to do something. But I watch, thoughts flowing through my tired head about what to say and what to do. Why am I here? Why am I involved?

Darren and Sarah, the girl who said she hated him. And maybe she did. Whatever happened between them yesterday, whatever fall out, is resolved. Darren and her being Quinn and my mum in a way. The idea that fall-out and make-up is some normal existence in life. Relationships defined by how you make up and not by why you fall out. Whatever words they threw at each other are now just sitting at the back of their memory ready to be thrown out when anger rises again. They haven't resolved the problem, they have just stopped the travel to the conclusion and peace, they have decided to go back to the beginning and not settle what is a fundamental flaw.

There is something there but I don't know if there is health inside, just two messed-up kids seeing a mirror of what they hate in themselves. If they can help someone like them, then maybe they can help themselves. If they can see something beautiful in the person who people think they are, then maybe there is beauty inside. I don't know the thoughts nor the reasons. Maybe it is just people want to be with someone and those who stick around with people like us are the people who understand because they are the same, and the hate we feel for ourselves is the only emotion that comes out when pushed. There sure seems to be a lot of unhappy people in the world.

I have lost concentration, I am stood in light, looking down when I should be staring at the light from closed windows. I look again and the house is darker. Rooms where light had been now black rectangles in the brick.

What am I waiting for? I think, when the question should be What do I do? I need help, someone with authority and voice, but someone who will listen and here I am at the gate to the house where a teacher lives. I flick the latch and the creak of a hinge and a spring and the old wood make a noise that seems loud in the silence. I walk the path to the front door, slower than I can, giving myself every chance to back away and run, to be the coward and just wait it out and see what happens and react and lie the best way I can to find the easiest place to stay unnoticed.

I walk forward and knock on the door, which opens immediately, light flying out and making me blink.

"I didn't think you'd build up the courage to come," Mrs. Brooke says.

I stare because whatever picture my subconscious had created for what could be, this was not one.

She laughs a little, confident and without fear.

"I've been watching you there, like you wanted to be caught all out in the open. Didn't actually think you'd get the nerve to come up here."

I don't think about why she is here, or why she has opened the door, or why she is speaking to me.

"Is Mr. Hutton here?" I ask.

She smiles at my voice and words.

"Come in," she tells me. "We can wait for him. I wasn't planning on going to bed till he is back anyways."

She leads me into the front room where there is no TV but a fire that is burning and soft chairs and a feeling that the only people that like this space are old and desire the quiet peace of being left alone.

"You need something to eat or drink?" she asks.

I shake my head.

She stands and watches me, waiting for me to speak but I have nothing to say and it is only now that I am trying to understand why she is here.

"Have a seat Billy," she tells me.

I don't put up a fight and I melt into a large red leather armchair that moulds itself to me like I have pushed into warm snow.

"Is she okay?" Mrs. Brooke asks.

"Sarah?"

She nods.

"It's important I know," she says.

"She's okay."

"She with someone?"

I nod, not wanting to say but knowing I must.

"Darren," I tell her.

She nods and snorts quietly in humour.

"She always chooses the controversy. Is she safe?" she says again.

"They are together. Have been a while I think."

She nods and looks to the window that is drawn and nothing to give a view nor reflection.

"Was hoping it would be someone else," she says. She turns to me, "He okay?"

I shake my head.

"He's in trouble."

"Yes, he is," she says. "Maybe more than you think."

"He says it wasn't him."

"Not many people admit to murder," she says.

There is nothing to say, I can't convince.

"You are sure she is okay? Safe?" she asks again.

"Darren is a lot of things, some of them, the bad ones, maybe aren't true. Sarah went to help him. They are just waiting, quietly. That's all."

"Do you know where?"

"I know where they said they'd be, where they said they'd stay. They aren't running. They aren't stupid enough to think they can vanish."

"They aren't doing anything stupid?"

I shake my head.

"And you are waiting for Jim. Mr. Hutton?"

I nod.

"You are going to tell him? Speak to him?"

I nod again.

She looks up, her mind racing, probably thinking of grabbing me and shaking me and beating information out so she can do something other than wait.

"Do you promise me she is safe?"

"She is safe. Darren wouldn't let anything bad happen. Not to her. And they aren't doing anything to each other, or themselves. It's not what they are thinking."

She doesn't relax, doesn't calm, but she is hiding it well. She sits down in the other armchair, and pulls a book from the small table at its side. She opens it, looks over its top at me and reads.

22.30 p.m.

I hear the door, the key and the turn and then the push and the step. I hear the voices and recognise them both. Mr. Hutton is talking to Serge, and the short replies of, "I know," and "Okay," are all Serge says. There is a deference in him, one I have never heard.

Mrs. Brooke puts her book down, looks to me, "Stay there," she says.

So I do, sat down, my hands resting on the leather arms, sat back but up right, like I'm riding the world's most comfortable roller coaster. I hear Mrs. Brooke whisper, the words of Mr. Hutton cut down. I don't know what she says but the room is full of three other people before I can understand anything.

Serge stays back but he is looking at me. Here, in his home he doesn't have the rule or the place. I think he has lied, or held information back and Mr. Hutton knows. Mrs. Brooke looks between them, never at me. She has watched me for a long time and has learned all she wants.

Mr. Hutton steps toward me, his face serious in the way he carries his emotions at school. He looks stern but not scary. He is a serious man who demands honesty.

"Are you going to speak, Billy?" he asks.

I nod, but I'm looking around the room, scared again, not sure with what I am doing. But I have trapped myself in a house, with a promise to people who care and one I am scared I will betray.

"He'll already know most of what you say," Serge says. "I'll protect myself. I haven't lied," he says.

"But he hasn't told me anything either, not what I need. He knows that," Mr. Hutton says. "Not speaking doesn't mean you haven't lied, it just means you have made a promise to someone else and that isn't always a good thing."

Mr Hutton turns to me.

"I'd like to know some things, Billy. Why you are here, and where your brother is, and, from what I gather, that would also be where Sarah is."

"Can I trust you?" I ask.

"You made that decision already by coming here. I take it as the compliment it is. But don't be naïve enough to think I don't have anything in this game. I do. More than you know. I need to be sure Sarah is safe."

"She is with Darren."

"Which is not the assurance I'm looking for nor the guarantee you seem to believe it is. Sarah, as you have experienced today makes decisions that are sometimes deliberately damaging, self-harming, and others that she just doesn't know why she has done them but the result is the same. If she were going to choose anyone from this town to make people question her sanity, your brother would be that person."

"He seemed different," Serge says.

Mr. Hutton turns to face Serge again.

"We all seem different at different times. We can all act in moments. But what we are is seen in patterns. Darren has patterns that concern a lot of people. The police being among them which is why they are looking for him."

Serge nods and looks down at the floor. It isn't fear it is knowledge he has spoken out of turn to a man who knows more and is more, a man who won't act on a whim.

"Is Sarah with him?" he asks me.

I nod.

"And why is it that you need to trust me?" he adds.

"He said she was safe," Mrs. Brooke tells him.

"What he means is that Darren - presumably young and loved up because who wouldn't feel great having the attention of Sarah? - is no danger to her. And that I have no doubt is correct. Although I have been wrong multiple times today. But what he isn't, is a person able to stop Sarah making terrible decisions. Those decisions she makes because she feels it will be exactly the wrong thing to do. Like running from school today."

"Darren wasn't there for Billy," Mrs. Brooke says.

"I was getting to that conclusion myself," Mr. Hutton says. "Darren also wasn't there to break Crane's nose, but he did all the same. And Sarah went to the party despite being told that she couldn't."

"She snuck out," Mrs. Brooke says. "She wasn't the first."

"I didn't know," Serge tells them.

"You just didn't want to think," Mr. Hutton tells him. "Which brings us back to you Billy. I saw you at your home, saw what you saw, in fact I saw more. I understand why you ran, I would have too. I'm guessing you have spoken to Darren. Is my trust needed there?"

"He didn't do it," I say.

"That is a possibility, but police and judges and scientists will decide those things. There is a significant amount of explaining and honesty to go on. But, right now, knowing you are here and safe is a wonderful relief. But I also need to make sure that Sarah is also that way."

"I can take you to them," I say.

"Or you could tell me and many people could get there quickly, wherever there is, and we can start the process of making all this make sense in some way. I'm not at all sure Sarah is safe, not in what I know of her."

"They didn't ask me to come here," I say.

"But you are, and I imagine they didn't ask anyone anything. I imagine Sarah wouldn't accept help from anyone, and while my experience of Darren is limited to his behaviour at school, I can't think he would be willing to accept help either."

"They don't know what to do," I say.

"Because the thing they need to do is the thing they refuse. They need to stand up and take responsibility and consequence."

"I need you to help them," I say.

"Billy, I have been run around all day. Darren comes to my school, assaults a teacher, the police visit and you are difficult. You run with a young lady who is in my legal guardianship, I am called to a murder scene because the police think I can somehow have an insight into a student and an ex student. They think I will know things as if I can read minds. A young man who lives under my roof is arrested at a beach party and I have to go and get him while I find out the young lady has once again run away and this time with the one person, and I am sorry to say this, who I would not want her speaking to let alone being in a relationship with. The police want to question him about the murder of his father. So Billy, I don't know who you think I am or what I am able to do. But I need you to tell me where Sarah is currently hiding so I can do something to remedy the situation."

"I need to look after my brother."

Mr. Hutton exhales loudly and lowers his head. He looks at the floor. He runs his left hand through his hair.

"I think I am something of who you imagine me to be. Not all of it because that simply can't be. I will come with you and I will speak and I will be honest. But that is all I can tell you. My concerns are not the same as yours. Possibly they overlap, maybe they work together. I don't know."

I stand up, small still, but bigger than before.

"I just need you to listen, to make sure whatever Darren says is heard. That's all."

22.55 p.m.

He promised me nothing, refused to give his word beyond telling me he needed to see and speak. He offered to drive but I told him it is better to walk. So I take them along the roads they know and going the way they will have walked hundreds of times before.

"They in the tunnel?" Mr. Hutton asks.

I don't answer, I just keep walking and they follow because while they are sure where we are heading there is always that doubt they are wrong. Mr. Hutton, Mrs. Brooke and Serge follow, and they are not speaking, not looking at each other, just keeping pace with me. Mr. Hutton has brought a torch to see, Mrs. Brooke to calm, and Serge as a physical defence. Were he younger I think he would have told them to stay. I smile at what I saw in his house. The interaction, the gentle touches, the looks and the smiles. I had wanted to ask Mrs. Brooke why she was there but it was obvious from photos and the way they all spoke and knew of each other that she lives there, that her and Hutton are a couple. For a moment I thought of siblings and I don't know why, it shouldn't be difficult to see them together, but I did. But the way they are together, the way they move, the concern and respect in held back anger and calmer words tells me everything.

"Why doesn't everyone know about you two?" I ask.

"Because no one wants to see," Hutton says. "I'm a grumpy old man who is obviously single. No need to say otherwise."

"How long?" I ask, and I know this is nerves, this is me trying to drag out a moment and their answers are the same, trying to keep me on board, trying to keep me going.

"Since about a week after I started at school," Mrs. Brooke says. "So twenty years, almost."

I don't look back, I don't want to know the looks they are exchanging. I want to believe in what I think, in what I want to know.

"Sarah knows?" I ask.

They laugh but I don't look. I know it is a stupid thing to say, but I want words not silence, I need connection rather than fear. I don't know if I am doing the right thing or if I am doing it the right way. They are humouring me, or playing along. I'm sure of this.

"She lives there, of course she knows," Serge says.

"But she didn't say."

"None of us do, just seems to be the way of it," Mrs. Brooke tells me.

23.20 p.m.

The tunnel is dark but Mr. Hutton doesn't take the lead. I walk first and he switches on the torch behind me. Light passes and I can see the walls and the ceiling clearly, my own shadow bouncing around in front like a long black arrow shaking in direction. We walk and the voices stop, footsteps reverberate and that wet echo rings out. Our footsteps are not in time, and they clatter and slap the concrete in random, non-repeating noise. We walk and we make the turns and I see the end of the tunnel as the light from the torch breaks through. I can see the light from the fire that still burns on the beach, as it flickers and spits flames at varying intensity. It is bigger and brighter than when I left which means only one thing and I see as I walk out onto the steps down, being careful not to slip on the wet algae. Darren and Sarah are sat close to the fire, the wood depleted in stock, and they are facing me, and they unlock their cuddle, their hug for warmth and closeness and they stand and watch us all walk over in silence, each of us struggling with the sand, and Mr. Hutton not turning off his light.

"Are you Okay Sarah?" Mrs. Brooke asks.

I can hear her kindness, the gruff hard woman a bluff of sorts, but real when needed.

Sarah smiles and nods. "I'm good," she says.

Darren is looking at everyone there, from one face to the next.

"This your plan?" he asks me.

"You can't run away, but you need to go in without a fight," I say. "You need someone to speak for you."

"And you think that will be me?" Mr. Hutton asks.

"They listen to you, the police. They call you, ask your opinion. Get you involved."

"They called me for you. They called me later for Serge. No one was asking my opinion of Darren, most people already have one and it isn't good."

"But yours is different," I say.

"Is it? I don't think so. I've taught a lot of kids, seen a lot of things, and I know you have it hard, I know, believe me. But Darren was nothing but who he wanted to be."

"There was no other way he could be," I say.

"That is something on which we will have to disagree," Mr. Hutton says.

He turns to Darren.

"You seem to be in quite some trouble," he tells him. "Which despite Billy's words is not really my concern. Sarah, however is very much."

"He didn't do anything wrong. I made the choice. Just me," Sarah says, her voice higher pitched as if Hutton is a judge.

"I'm sure you did Sarah, just like you make most of your decisions. They are ultimately yours. But what fuels them, what makes you decide is not alone in your head."

He turns his head slowly to face her.

"You make poor choices, and the reasons why don't need to be explained again. But as we have spoken many times, this doesn't have to mean you crash through life not caring about yourself."

"I haven't done anything wrong," Darren says.

Hutton turns to him, the light pointed at the floor.

"You broke Mr. Crane's nose," he says. "You caused chaos in my school. You have brought Sarah into this, and most importantly for the law, you are a suspect in your father's killing."

"It wasn't me."

"Which are the words of most guilty people."

We stand and no one moves, two sides facing and I am with the wrong group. I step across, reach out and touch Darren's upper arm. He smiles and nods, but doesn't look into my eyes.

"What is it exactly you would like me to do, Darren? Lie for you? Represent you in a way that isn't truthful? What?" Hutton asks.

"He just needs someone there to stop what is coming," I say. "They won't give him a chance, they won't be soft. And he'll fight and that will cause more."

"What are you going to tell them, Darren?" Hutton asks.

Darren scrunches his face, twitches muscles and swallows.

"See, you can't do it," Hutton tells him. "You are thinking of lies you could tell, lies no one would believe. The truth is the only thing that works in life, and in this right here, everything that has happened, you have to tell the truth."

Darren looks up and stares at Hutton. I can see the anger because it isn't hidden. Quinn would laugh now, looking at his son whose frustration from an inability to do anything to change the situation, knowing that lashing out would only result in a beating. The impotency of being the victim.

"I could have stopped it," Darren says.

Sarah twists her head quickly to look at Darren's face. He knows but he stares ahead, looking into the distance rather than the people.

"I know I could have," he says again.

Darren pauses, lost in his head, trying to understand if we will be happy with only knowing this much. It is a futile process because what he says will have to be repeated many times as people look for holes in his story.

"Go on," Mr. Hutton tells him.

"Me and Sarah, we fell out last night, argued."

"You okay?" Mrs. Brooke asks Sarah again.

"I look after myself," Sarah says.

"Not what I asked," Mrs. Brooke tells her.

"We fell out with words," Sarah continues. "Nothing more. And I did the talking. Darren just took it, which is the problem. He just stood and took it all and then walked off. That wasn't right."

"Then how did you know to meet up today?" Mr. Hutton asks.

"Because we always do," Darren says. "Same place same time. And tonight there was this party, and then things changed and I needed to speak to her and I didn't think she'd be here, and I just messed up."

"You came to the school to see Sarah?" Mrs. Brooke asks.

"I'm sorry about that. I, well . . I had taken something, some amphetamine – dumb thing to do, I know. I'm sorry. I just did. I needed something, something I thought would give me the edge on Quinn. I walked away in the morning and I just wanted to get back and not be a coward anymore."

"And you went to see him anyway?" Mrs. Brooke asks Sarah.

"I needed to know," Sarah says. "Billy told me something and I needed to know. I knew he'd be there, so I went and he told me."

"Told you what?" Mr. Hutton asks.

"What happened," Darren says.

"Which is where we need to be. I believe Serge has covered for you all, not through lying but simply not having the capacity to remember. I am not sure if this is some type of principle on his part or a simple need not to incriminate. I am very quickly moving to the latter."

"I could only guess. I don't know anything," Serge says.

"You have heard and seen plenty. Did you know, for instance that Sarah was in a relationship with Darren?"

Serge doesn't look anywhere but down.

"I figured she was seeing someone," he says. "I wouldn't have believed it to be him."

"But it is. And we are here," Hutton tells him.

"It is not what you think," Sarah says.

"And what is it that I would be thinking?" Mr. Hutton asks.

"Another older guy, another bad man, and me all innocent and stupid."

"People have patterns, Sarah."

"Nothing has happened," Darren says. "Nothing like what you are thinking."

"What I am thinking is how to end all this quickly, and that seems to be to call in the police and let them sort out everything that has happened according to whoever has said or done what. That isn't my job."

There is silence, Hutton's words and the weight of his voice along with his history of power make us all look down. But I can't hold my gaze at the flickers of light on the sand.

"Let him talk," I say. "And from there see what we do. You can't condemn someone on what you think they are, only on what has happened."

Hutton stares at me, the anger in him not something I have seen before from him. And in honesty it isn't the anger Quinn would show. It is different in that I don't feel scared. Maybe this is him or maybe me. Maybe in the moment or in life I can't be scared, not like before. Quinn is gone and maybe the terror he held is no longer present anywhere.

"You give everyone a chance, always," I say. "Darren deserves to speak, to have you listen to decide if what he says makes sense, whether it makes him innocent."

Hutton watches me and rubs his tongue between his upper lip and teeth, the skin bulging and moving like an animal has burrowed across.

"You have your audience, Darren. Let's hear what you have to say."

Darren looks nervous, everyone looking at him, everyone in dark with a fire burning. From a distance it would seem some religious ritual of pagan design.

"Quinn blew up in the morning. Billy was there. I guess you know that. We fought. Me and Quinn. I thought I had him, and I did but I let it go and he put me down like he always does. He was breathing hard though, I could see it in his eyes and face how close I had come and how he knew he got lucky. I should have done one thing and I didn't because I was scared, scared I'd win and then it would just be worse. Not that it can be worse. Not worse than this. I left and I guess Billy got some too," Darren looks at me. "I've taken some hidings for you over the years, stepped in and taken the beating, I guess you got one because of me today." He looks back down, smiling in a memory of something I don't know.

"I went out, ran really, thinking I'd go to work, but I knew I wouldn't. I thought about it on the way in, thought about how I had him and blew it, how I'd take him next time, how I knew I could. I figured he'd drink in celebration, or drink in something, and that edge he had would fade away. He isn't as good when drunk, not as strong. And I knew he was going to run away. I had some speed, just a little, a bit more than I thought. I haven't done much of that for a while, no need and no time, I guess. But I did and I skipped work, just didn't show, and I walked about, coming up and feeling strange in that way that should be good but isn't. I walked around, feeling better in some ways, stronger, more confident, my heart going. I didn't have any plan, I just wanted another go. I thought about Sarah and what had happened, how I walked away from that too, how I always walk away. Billy is the same. It's the only way it works. I've won some fights but my reputation is just through anger, nothing I can do. Serge put me on my arse more times than I remember. I guess he is here to protect you from me. It isn't needed. That isn't happening."

He pauses, taking a breath, trying to remember what he has said. Remembering what comes next.

"I went back home, figuring I'd take another shot, make sure he knew I was going to keep coming. Quinn weaker and me, in my mind, stronger for the drugs. It didn't make sense then and it doesn't now. I know that. I walked home, trying to stay out of everyone's way, trying not to be seen, but people did. There isn't anything you can do around here without it being known. Plenty would have seen me walk back. I waited outside for a long time, or what seemed long to me. Walked up and down, talked myself out of it a couple of times too. Talked myself back in though. One of them things, if I can convince a little more then I'm not involved at all. None of it happens."

"If what you are saying is true, then with or without you Quinn dies," Mr. Hutton says.

Darren looks down and nods, but it isn't agreement just a recognition that this thought is one he will have to hear, one he will have to acknowledge and accept.

"I just walked in and whatever I thought was going to happen didn't. I thought Quinn would be there, shouting or making fun, or laughing, but he didn't. He just looked at me and he knew why I was back. He didn't say anything, didn't do what he normally does. He looked at my hands, looked to see if I was carrying anything and I wasn't. It was Billy's mum who did the shouting. A real anger, she pushed me, tried to push me out the door. She told me where I should be, that I shouldn't be there. That I hadn't needed to come back. Wasn't one kicking enough for one day? Could I not just leave them to be happy? But it never is one beating, just one is rare. At least it used to be.

"Quinn stood and tried to push past me, but I pushed back and he smiled and tried his routine. I don't know what had happened, maybe it was me, maybe he knew the morning had been the last time. I don't know, that's what I thought, and think. He knew. He told me he didn't have time, he was going out. And he was. I asked if he was going for drink or to meet up with his other lady. He laughed and your mum did too, Billy. Only I said her name, because I knew. And your mum knew too. This is too small a town and too many people who want to try and hurt with words. I'd heard it all, and your mum had too. Just no one had dared say it loud till then."

He looks at me, and I think he believes there is something there, something I should feel. Maybe he thinks I should attack him for accusations. He looks at me as if checking I am giving my blessing to continue. I smile and nod, and he nods back.

"Quinn laughed, tried to wipe it away. But I told him about times and dates from the last two weeks, where he'd gone with her, what he was trying to do, and he was trying to get out, trying to move on, trying to find someone else to suck the life out of."

"Who is it?" Mr. Hutton asks.

And Darren tells him.

"She has nothing but a house with broken windows," Serge says.

"But it is a place where I won't be and where Billy can't go, and where there is something new, and something he'd see as fresh. There would be other reasons too, debt most likely one, or simple hate the other, but he was making moves to get away. He was already going. You can make your own guesses at why. I wasn't going and he wanted away from me. I don't know the whys, I just know he was going."

"You don't know that," Mr. Hutton says.

"I don't know, but I said the stuff and Quinn couldn't speak, and he wasn't fighting, and he just smiled at me, and he smiled at your mum, and he tried to push me again, but I pushed back and he went staggering. And fell on his arse. I put him down, Billy, right there on the carpet on his arse. I put him down. In the front room, sat there trying to get up but struggling. He did the whole anger thing, his face going and his eyes, but he didn't come charging or swinging, he just stared at me and smiled and told me all the things he had already said to me a thousand times. He told me how he hated me, how I was nothing, how could a man like him be proud of a nothing like me? He told me that I could do whatever I wanted, go or stay or do whatever because he was done. He didn't have a son, he didn't have anything. All of this is over, he said."

He waits for someone to tell him something, maybe scold him, tell him how dumb he had been. But we all wait, wanting the next part, wanting to know.

"Your mum started with the screaming, insulting that woman, insulting your dad, and Quinn didn't lash out, didn't insult back, he just laughed at your mum, shrugged, said nothing. That was worse. He didn't care, never had. She saw it. He was a coward, walking away into a new set-up because the one he had was collapsing. He could kick me out, but there would be the fight and the loss of money, and then there's you, Billy. He was pretty stuck there. Not a lot to do other than slap you now and again. That balance, he could never go too far, could he? Not with you. If he did there was always the danger he'd have to go."

Darren looks up and we are listening and waiting, thinking that nothing means anything at all.

"I wouldn't let him leave," Darren says, his voice quieter. "I kept pushing him in the chest and he was just taking it. There was nothing there, no aggression, no threats, just a smile and a laugh. He told me he didn't care, he would never fight me again, that none of anything I did mattered at all. I looked at him and he wasn't going to do anything but walk, walk away. A complete coward."

Darren looks at me again and his smile is faked.

"Your mum came back, I didn't realise she had gone. She asked me to move out the way, pushed me too. She used the hand she was carrying the knife. You'll know the one, the one she always used, the only one she would sharpen. She pushed past with it and Quinn saw and Quinn laughed. He told her to pack it in, stop being daft and she waved it about not knowing what she was doing. She'd done it before, certainly looked that way, but always an empty threat. Quinn was laughing at us, more her than me. He stepped up and he shouted, used the woman's name, told her what I'd said was true. Said it could have been any number like he was some catch, but it was her. I moved out the way, stepped back, and your mum lashed out, slashed him and he held up his hand and she cut that. He grabbed at her and she just started stabbing. I watched, stepping away. She got his neck pretty quick, it just opened and he knew and he stared and she didn't stop, she just kept going. Wouldn't stop, couldn't."

Darren is looking at us now, needing us to do or say something but I don't know what, I don't have any words, nothing to say.

"What did you do, Darren?" Mrs. Brooke asks.

"I ran. I got out and I ran. I checked for blood on me as best I could. I ran and then I stopped and I saw it all again. The blood, the knife, the cuts. I saw it. I knew Quinn was dead. I knew I was there, I knew I could have stopped it. I could have stepped in, I could have done something, not said something, or anything. But I did nothing, I just watched, edging away, and making me as guilty as anyone. What can I do about that?"

We stand in silence on the secluded beach thinking of what Darren has told us. I try and picture the scene, try to run it through my mind. My mother a killer because Quinn was going, the only witness was Darren.

"Billy's mother has another story," Hutton says.

"I don't doubt she does. She innocent in it?" Darren asks.

"Not as much as she thinks," Hutton tells him.

"Does she have Darren holding the knife?" I ask. "Darren doing the killing?"

"That she does," Hutton says.

"You ever touch the knife, Darren?"

"Not today. Not for a long time."

"You are taller than her too. A lot more. The cuts won't match up. If it wasn't you," I say, wanting to trust.

"Still can't believe me," Darren says.

"Just the questions that will need to be answered. Not by you, or by word. By science and all that." I tell him.

"You actually believe in all that?" he asks.

"Seems to be the way it all works. They'll have to bring people in to examine, see what they can read from it all," I say. "If what you say is true then you just have to tell your truth and wait."

"I'd have to trust them to try and find the answers."

"My mum isn't smart enough to lie her way through. She will have already made mistakes, she will already have forgotten some of what she has said."

Darren looks to Sarah and she smiles back at him.

"Mr. Hutton?" Darren asks.

"I can't say anything better than Billy. If what you say is what actually happened then the police will figure that out quick enough."

"They think I'm guilty?" Darren asks.

"Some do. I certainly did," Hutton tells him.

"And now?"

"Now I have my doubts. But I'm not one who gets to decide. The truth is there and it is easy to find. You can't run away and there is no point ending it all over something you haven't done."

Darren looks down again and Sarah steps to him and pushes his upper arm and he laughs.

"What do you think?" he asks.

"I think you should do what I don't nearly often enough and go with Jim," she says. "And make sure you tell the truth. No lies, no adding stuff because you think it's better, makes a better story. Stick to what you saw and heard. Don't be guessing at other things."

Darren looks up to the sky and takes a deep breath and blows it out into the air.

"I didn't choose any of this," he says.

"Nobody ever does," I tell him.

Midnight

We walk back, Hutton telling us we need to sit and wait at his house while he calls in the police. Spending a night in sleep would be disrespectful and only provide more time to think and doubt what we agreed. Mrs. Brooke walks with Sarah, her arm wrapped around the girl with the red hair for the first minute, walking ungainly and with difficulty but providing a closeness of touch. Sarah doesn't fight back. We walk through the tunnel,

Hutton's light shining the way and no one talking. We have accepted - and Darren most of all - that this is what needs to be done. I am thinking, like we all are, about Darren's words, about his story, about what he thinks he saw. I think it is true, and there is the possibility he has left out events, or seen things not as they were but as he wants. This is always the way. Memory isn't perfect, especially when under stress.

We all sit and wait once we are inside. Mrs. Brooke and Sarah close, Serge stood in the corner of the room, not really seeming to belong, not understanding his use. Darren stands up when Mr. Hutton makes the call. He asks for a specific person, is put through, and tells them Darren is in his house and ready to come in. He places the phone down and we wait. But not for long. They arrive without lights flashing or sirens blaring, Mr. Hutton had told them to be quiet. There is a knock at the door and we all exchange looks as this is the last of us as a group. We came together briefly, shared an experience and now it is over.

The police walk in and Darren nods, he looks relaxed or at least not on heightened emotion and ready to fight. They exchange words and they tell him his rights. Anything you do say and all that.

Darren stops at the door and turns and looks to me.

"See you, Billy," he says, and I smile and say nothing back.

Two years later.

I didn't think I would come, didn't think I had the need. But I do or I wouldn't be here. I'm eighteen and legally a man. I can choose what I do and where I go and who I see. The only barriers are the law, not that there are any to prevent all this. I didn't think I'd ever come. The last two years have been something I would call life, something I can look back on and describe as growing up.

I stayed that night at Mr. Hutton' house. I stayed there till now, and I still have a place, a room with him and Mrs. Brooke and the kids he has come through. I got my apprenticeship and I work with wood. Two years of one day at college and a salary that doesn't pay for a thing, certainly not a holiday as I worked the other four. But I earn now, more than before, not enough to be independent, not enough to buy a place of my own. Serge has moved on, a town nearby and he visits most weekends and he plays pool and he wins, and we chat and he is older and smarter not dumber. Still single and still cool.

The prison is a place a hundred miles away, and I came by train because I still can't drive although I think I will, soon too, if I can get the money together. They like the youngest to do the driving, particularly in the afternoon, probably because a couple of them drink. But I can't yet and they make fun, like they always do, but it is easier than anything Quinn threw my way. I didn't go to the funeral, haven't been up to the grave and never will, I can't see a reason to do it. Darren was the same. I don't know who went, and I don't care. I haven't asked, and don't want to find out.

My mother lied, and kept on going. Then lied to cover lies and the science made her guilty. She blamed Darren, then she said he was involved, then she said he planned it, made her do it. She never admitted guilt, never said she did it for any other reason than she was forced. She blamed Quinn for abuse. She tried everything, tried to throw any story at people who would listen. None of them stuck and she was found guilty, and Darren was free, innocent, his story holding up, but people in the town not believing it all. He was Quinn's son and he had to have some guilt. It was another story to add to a reputation he didn't want, couldn't fulfil and would hang around him for as long as people gossip. He said it just made people leave him alone. People thought he had killed and managed to get free and no one wants to fight a psycho. But he isn't, and never was.

Darren came back after he left with the police that night, two days away and he stayed with Mr. Hutton. A week in total and he was quiet, and him and Sarah spoke sometimes. He and Serge played pool, and not many words were exchanged. They set him up with his own place and he had to pay a fine for breaking Crane's nose. Hutton set him up with work, and he labours on sites, sometimes we cross paths, but not often. We chat when we do.

Him and Sarah didn't last, not that they really started. They were cool, I guess, or appeared to be. She came to college too, learned how to do hair, or learned more as she said. She is still around as well, but living with friends in the city down the coast. She pops by but less than Serge. We never talk about that night.

So I am here, having passed through security in a female prison to see the woman they still call my mother. I wait, am scanned and searched and led to a room with a plastic chair attached by a metal frame to a plastic table and a chair on the other side. They lead her in and she looks older, which she is, but better, which she isn't. Healthier as the days of hedonism are long since gone. She doesn't smile when she sees me, and I don't when I look at her. She shuffles across and sits opposite and the guards stand back and watch and listen. She has sent me three letters and I read each of them, but only once, before I put them in the bin. She lied and tried for emotion and tried to tell me things that weren't true. They were words she knew would be read by others, words she wanted and needed others to believe, to make her stay shorter, or better, or to make people believe she was the victim. Some should have hurt, some should have meant something. But it didn't.

I had thought of her, of my life, of my childhood. Of her and Quinn, of the life and the house and the beatings and the words and the future they cared nothing about. I thought about me and what I was and I am and what I will be. She asked three times for me to visit, for her to explain. But I don't need her to lie, I don't need to try and sift through her self-pity and manipulation of what happened.

But I am here now because I want to visit. I organised this, and she agreed. I don't know what she thinks and there was a part of me that thought she would sit in her cell and hide and not come. But there she is, her face older but softer, staring at me, and not knowing whether to smile.

"I didn't think I'd see you again," she says.

We have sat and stared at each other for a minute, playing a game of power. But I won as soon as I came because she needs me and I do not need her.

"That had been the plan," I say.

"But you are here."

"Not for as long as you."

"I killed Quinn," she says.

I nod because this is something we all know.

"I did it for us," she adds and I laugh.

"You did it because he was leaving you. And you blamed everyone but yourself."

She smiles at this and nods and looks down and then up.

"How is Darren?" she asks.

"He is doing really well," I say.

"That's good," she tells me. "What is he doing?"

"He doesn't want you to know."

I told him I was coming here to see her, and he told me he couldn't understand why. He told me not to tell her anything about him. His life is his and sharing anything with her would dilute that to a point that he didn't care to see.

"Tell him I'm sorry," she says.

"I'm not going to lie for you," I tell her.

"Why did you come?"

"I don't know. I thought it was to let you see me as I am. To see you as you are. To make sure there is nothing there, and there isn't. I think I just wanted to tell you thank you. Thank you for teaching me what matters, what I am. Maybe none of that at all. Maybe I just wanted to come and see you were suffering. I was waiting to feel something, I don't know if that was positive or negative. But right now just a little curiosity."

"You are speaking different," she says.

"I never used to speak because no one used to listen."

"I made a lot of mistakes."

"Too many to come back from."

"I've changed."

"That's a good thing but the past hasn't."

"I'm your mother," she says.

"If that's what you want to call yourself, go ahead. Don't expect it from me."

"We had good times."

"I had good times, me alone. Quinn ended that. You and Quinn put and end to it. But now it is back, not always, but often."

"Do you not want to hear what I have to say?"

"Is any of it true?"

She watches me, her eyes narrowing. The effort she was putting in ebbing away as she sees the futility of it all.

"Why are you here?"

"For no reason at all."

Printed in Great Britain
by Amazon